V

An Anthology

Writers in Stone

Also by Writers in Stone

Driftwood: An Anthology (2019)

Cuckoo: An Anthology (2021)

Lock and Key: An Anthology (2022)

Seventy Three (2022)

First Edition
ISBN: 9798882989346

Cover design: Wings of Weston Photography

Interior Artwork: Bari Sparshott (Otis)

The copyrights © for their contributions remain with the authors, who have asserted their moral rights to be so identified under the Copyright, Design and Patent Act 1988. All rights reserved.

Contents

Introduction 7

Social Media

Cyberspace	Ann Bunn	11
Social Media	Macaque	12
Linking Up	Ann Bunn	13

Extract

The Sea Gives and the Sea Takes…	Elizabeth Lawrence	17
Shadows of the Cinnamon Apple Trees	Lois Elsden	22
Dressing Up	Brian Price	24
Poet's Retreat	Macaque	25

Crime

A Peculiar Sighting	Brian Price	29
Crime View	Lois Elsden	32
_Honesty	Macaque	37

Doctor

Doctor Chivers	Lois Elsden	43
Doctor	Elizabeth Lawrence	46
Time for the Doctor	Brian Price	49
When the Doctor Calls	Simon Phelps	52
Doctor in the House	Elizabeth Lawrence	58
Wrecking Ball	Macaque	61

Rope

Ruth	Fenja Hill	67
An Unintended Consequence	Brian Price	71
Rope	Elizabeth Lawrence	73

Down by the River	Macaque	77
Rope	Lois Elsden	83

Proverb

Oliver Patterson's Adventurous Year	Simon Phelps	87
Another Turned Page	Lois Elsden	94
A Stitch in Time Saves Nine	Elizabeth Lawrence	96
The Customer is Always Right	Macaque	99
Need to Know	Brian Price	101

Recording

For the Record	Macaque	107
Water my Blood	Elizabeth Lawrence	111
Stone Tapes	Lois Elsden	119
A Slipped Disc	Brian Price	122

Revenge

The Water of Life	Fenja Hill	127
Payback	Brian Price	131
Best Served Cold	Lois Elsden	136
In the Bag	Macaque	138

Next

Customer Service	Brian Price	143
Mr Harland	Lois Elsden	145
Oxford, 1920	Macaque	148
Breaking the Silence	Fenja Hill	150

1000 Word Limit

Mole Vole and Duck	Lois Elsden	157
The Historians	Macaque	160

Crossed Words	Brian Price	163

Train

K'Homun Umbrakai	Macaque	169
What We Believe	Fenja Hill	172
Train from Hell	Brian Price	176
Homeward Bound	Lois Elsden	178

Something Found in a Book

My Dearest Emilia	Lois Elsden	183
Lamb for the Slaughter	Brian Price	185
Fields of Attraction	Macaque	188

Something Overheard

Café au Hate	Brian Price	195
Day Tripper	Macaque	197
Something Overheard	Lois Elsden	199

Cloak

In the Coppice Wood	Macaque	205
Cloak	Lois Elsden	209
Lost Property	Brian Price	211

Biographies	**215**
Index of Writers	**217**
Acknowledgements	**219**

Introduction

V is the fifth annual anthology by the Writers in Stone, a diverse group of writers who first met in the Rowan Tree Tea Rooms at the Old Quarry in Weston-super-Mare in the summer of 2017. The premise of the group was to get together at least once a month to encourage each other's writing and discuss their various projects and ideas. To combat writer's block, each meeting carries an optional theme to inspire a poem, short story, monologue or whatever takes a member's fancy, and it is a selection of the work presented on these themes that constitute the anthologies.

It has been wonderful to witness the development of the group and its members over the last seven years, with new publications and competition successes being celebrated at the meetings, as well as welcoming new members with different styles and visions. Please explore the other publications by individual members, and as with all local art or business, if you like something give it a great review on all your social media.

As always, the pieces in this anthology are edited only for uniformity of layout and typographical errors, not for content. We hope that any external readers will appreciate that all contributions are a mixture of fiction and memoir, and that our purpose in sharing them is to entertain and not to offend.

Macaque

Social Media

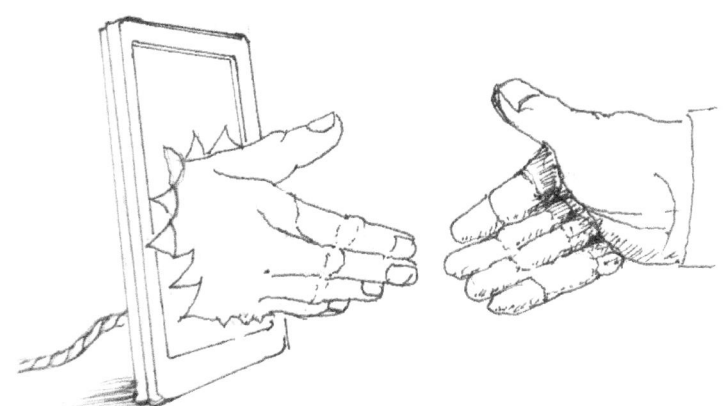

Cyberspace

Anne Bunn

I put up my profile on Facebook
My photo, my Ginger cat
I thought I'd just dip my toe in
I should have known better than that.

Before long, my scrolling was daily
Cyberworld clawed at my brain
Images became a compulsion
I'd boarded a runaway train!

Everyone wanted to 'friend' me
I was quite overwhelmed by it all
With entreaties from many a 'military' man
To chat, and engage and enthral.

Then came WhatsApp and Messenger
Instagram, Chat and Tik Tok
My poor little brain is exploding
There's aren't enough hours on the clock.

Now Chatbots are asking me questions
I've been hacked, and I'm over exposed
I look back with yearning to my younger days
When click bait left far less disclosed.

But my synapses are not yet rewired
So I can avoid most of the tripe
Two fingers to all algorithms
I'll decide what I want to swipe!

Social Media

Macaque

Pubs, gigs, team sports, the terraces,
Dinner tables, café tables, board games, a quiz,
Skate parks, country parks, theatres, drama groups,
Book clubs, nightclubs, back rubs, porch stoops,

Bonfire blazes, garden parties, BBQ's, fêtes,
Camping, hot tubs, Sunday strolls, kissing gates,
Church services, night school classes, train journeys,
Weekends away,
Exhibitions, galleries, talking points, having a say...

Even clapping for the NHS was a much better way
To socialise, participate, keep in touch and make someone's day
Than Facething, Instawhatnot, Twittybollocks, Snapaway,
All negative, divisive, antisocial media, if I may.

Linking Up

Anne Bunn

When you finally wake up to the fact that life has started to gallop by whilst you pootle along in its wake, you realise that it's time to embrace new horizons, scary though that may seem.

Acknowledging that, Jen had taken the first small step, becoming a wary participant in the somewhat intimidating world of social media.

At first, her circle of online friends was carefully limited to people she actually knew in the real world, then slowly expanded to those who shared mutual friends; keeping everything safe, stimulating and carefully appropriate for a woman well past her prime.

Her husband was unimpressed by her sudden enthusiasm for a world at the end of her phone, and glared darkly when he caught her engrossed in online conversation; anything not pertaining to him was viewed as an error in spousal duty, and therefore to be condemned out of hand.

Despite his disapproval, Jen continued her explorations in the unfamiliar, and decided to dip into the world of social networking, with Linkedin seeming to be an obvious choice for a retired teacher.

To her delight, she managed to re-engage with some old friends from college days, and the exchange of both professional and personal updates soon became an illuminating part of most evenings, keeping her mind active whilst her irascible husband shouted at television programmes.

It was about 3 months later that she stumbled across an education debate that she felt quite competent to contribute to, and was just about to wade in, when a posting from a new participant stopped her in her tracks.

The surname was an exceedingly common one, and his forename was equally mundane, but just seeing it was enough to make her mouth go dry, and having posted a 'like' to his comment, she logged out quickly, getting out the ironing board to re-focus on a non-emotional task.

She was determined to leave it there, let the past lie in peace, but next day, she logged in to follow the debate and there he was again, making exactly the points she would have posted.

Jen should have left it there; easier, less likely to cause any waves, but sometimes even the most logical of minds gives in to impulse, and now she had to know.

A quick click onto his profile, and there he was; the love of her young life, greying at the temples, an undeniably 'Dad' body now, but still that smile that took her straight back to her 19th summer.

Forcing herself to think 'professionally', she was pleased to note that he had had a very successful teaching career, but was he well, was he happy, did he even remember her?

There was no going back now, so she composed a carefully casual personal message, and sent it off into the ether before courage failed, or maybe common sense returned.

It was 3 agonising days before the reply came back. This was equally carefully crafted, but the main highlights were that he was separated, had 2 grown up sons, a small granddaughter, and how the hell could he have possibly forgotten her?

The build up of this relationship was to take time, willingness to trust and share, and much of it had to be conducted online due to their personal circumstances, but once the link was re-affirmed, they discovered that anything is possible if cyberworld is treated with caution and respect.

Five years on, and social media has taken over an increasingly jaded world. Jen is still cautious of the rabbit holes of social media, still wary of its dark allure, but as she smiles across the room at her 2nd husband, she is well aware that she has encountered its plus side too.

Extract

The theme for this month was to include the following two sentences from a translation of **L'Amant** by Marguerite Duras:

"*On the paths of the yard the shadows of the cinnamon-apple trees are inky black. The whole garden is still as marble.*"

The Sea Gives and the Sea Takes Away

Elizabeth Lawrence

"The way of water has no beginning and no end. The sea is around you and in you. The sea is your home before your birth and after your death. Our hearts beat in the womb of the world. Our breath burns in the shadows of the deep. The sea gives and the sea takes. Water connects all things. Life to death. Darkness to light". (**Avatar, The Way of Water**)

    The quiet village of Uphill is my home. Unique in its coastal proximity to the ancient limestone Mendips, where dramatic mounds and rolling hills are woven with rhynes and rivers that stretch to one of the fastest moving tides in the world, it has withstood many storms and gales from the Bristol Channel. The village is overlooked by a mighty hill, with an ancient beacon tower and Norman church on a steep-quarried cliff, which bore witness to the great tsunami of the early 17th century.
    Returning after many years, Uphill has so little changed that I often feel surrounded by memories and ghosts. I remember our garden, the old trees, knotted and gnarled. As children, we made swings and climbing ropes, the apple trees providing a fantasy world and refuge, where we learnt to climb in the safety of their strong branches. In teenage years, we propped cushions against their broad trunks and read summer afternoons away, chatting and dozing. And the sea, always the sea, just a few hundred yards away.
    I close my eyes and am back in that garden, one sunny winter's day in 1981. On the paths of the yard the shadows of the cinnamon-apple trees are inky black. The whole garden is still as marble. The trees are about to bear witness to an incredible force of nature.
    Such calm the night before the Great Flood, an eeriness as the motionless glassy sea waited with quiet prowess, like a monster in the dark, ready to pounce. The sound of the tide was discernible only by a whisper as it gently lapped onto the shore. I remember the sight, even now, so unusual was the stillness in the bay of the Bristol Channel. The calm before the storm, the silence broken only by occasional footsteps as folk made for home. I have wondered many times since how such tranquillity could possibly have been the

harbinger of danger. A full moon lingered, casting her silver spell onto the deep unfathomable surface.

The month of December had been peaceful so far. We had already decorated the house for Christmas, the tree twinkling and presents wrapped invitingly on the carpet beneath the richly-coloured glass baubles. We were snug indoors when the storm came, watching an old film while the dog snored in front of the fire. Wind and rain lashed against the sitting room window, scraping the rosebush thorns against the pane of glass, with squeals that made us shudder. Frequently, we would look out of the window at the willow tree's bare branches, its tentacles of concentric circles, coiled in a vortex of spinning gold as it wrapped around the diffused orange glow of the streetlamp, whipping the storm ever closer; we nonetheless felt safe and protected. Gazing from the delicate fairy lights on the Christmas tree to the violent flashing lights of the elements outside was an atmospheric contrast. The rain was heavy. Each time one of us went upstairs, we checked the street below. My sister reported that a river of rain was flowing rapidly down the road, pooling into a lake. We had never seen it so deep before.

Feeling uneasy, an instinct or a hunch made me look out of the front bedroom window to the sight of a wave surging up the driveway to our front door. Racing downstairs, relieved to see that water was not seeping through the letter box yet, I calmly but insistently told my mother and sister that we should now all go upstairs. Quick-thinking as ever, my mother took all the wrapped presents with her. I tucked our dog under one arm and a tin of biscuits under the other.

Before we had even reached the landing, the sea burst into every corner of our downstairs home and we were plunged into darkness. We watched from the window in disbelief as waves gushed down the road several feet deep, swaying and eddying as if we were on board a ship. Such darkness; black sea and a black sky without street lamps to show we lived on land. It was very disorienting and frightening. Our small, safe corner had been engulfed by treacherous water. Long before mobile phones, we had no communication with the outside world and no indication as to how deep the water would rise.

After about an hour, the situation seemed to have stabilised. Once news of the disaster had spread, we couldn't believe our eyes as the rescue traffic arrived in Uphill; instead of the usual sight of buses and cars on the road, there were rubber dinghies, canoes, rowing boats, speed boats, small yachts, and any seafaring vessels the helpers had to hand. We felt less alone now and heart-warmed by the response. My mother's partner arrived by boat from several miles away; "I knew he would come!" she said, with restored confidence and emotion in her voice. Many people were rescued from flooded homes and given beds and food in emergency centres. The water had receded, but a loud-hailer announced that everyone should evacuate as the next tide was predicted to be even higher. We decided to stay in our home and take a gamble on the water not reaching the upstairs, which thankfully it didn't. I had been wondering how feasible climbing onto the roof would have been.

The next morning broke, calm and sunny, as stunned residents surfaced to assess damage to property, themselves and each other. Wreckage was strewn everywhere and cars upturned. The WRVS, out in full-force, supplied the village with hot soup at lunchtime. After the seawater had drained away, the stench in homes was overpowering and rotting carpets were thrown out. All of our downstairs furniture, carpets and electrical goods were irretrievably damaged. Thankfully, our gas cooker still worked; we gathered around the flames on the hob for warmth and were able to cook hot meals. My mother, a single parent and running a hospital ward as staff nurse, went to work the next day, but as she was clearly still in shock, she was sent home. She suffered from PTSD for a while, but recovered as we rebuilt our future, stronger and wiser. Sandbags became a regular feature of village life for several months during high tides. There was so much help, support and community spirit for everyone. No one was left to struggle alone. Some people lost everything, but no lives were lost.

Uphill has not been flooded again. Strong structural sea defences have since been built, proving successful. A friend of mine, Ana Salote - author, climate activist and stalwart of the arts - co-produced an exhibition in 2022, which realistically showcased the disaster with photographs and emotional eye-witness testimonies. I was interviewed along with other flood survivors, and each one of us emphasised the same fact: "There was no warning!" One woman recounted checking on her baby asleep in his cot on the ground floor, when an instinct made her take him upstairs. Minutes later, a huge wave crashed into their house, the downstairs was several feet under water and the infant would have been submerged. The past was brought back to life in reconstructed flood-damaged homes, replicating every detail from the sea debris to the stench of decay, its familiar smell assailing my nostrils. It became part of a government documentary for Flood Action Week. We were asked if flooding could happen again. Most were confident this was a one-off and would not happen again in our lifetimes, albeit it more likely now with climate change. I replied, "the sea is a powerful force and nature has the last word."

***

Forty years later, one summer's day in the late afternoon, the sun's rays raced across Weston Bay, sparkling on the sea and Marine Lake. Wind and sunlight danced like diamonds on the surface of the rough sea. My friends and I splashed in the high waves, shrieking like children from the sheer exhilaration. Hungry for more, we walked across the long beach, barefoot on silky sand, to the lake. We dipped into the still coolness, sheltered from the rough sea by an island and causeway, and swam in the safe shallow, smiling at each other and at the sun. After climbing out, and pouring tea from our flasks, we sat on the warm slabs of stone around the apron of the lake, drying ourselves in the last warm rays, feeling mellow and tingly, gazing out towards the shimmering sea. Perhaps having tapped into our inner children, we reminisced about our upbringings in a very honest and emotional way, opening old wounds and empathising with each other. The summer wind seemed to disperse our sadness as we sat together, older now, but still those children. Strange, how this shared experience evoked such memories. I felt grateful to have these like-minded friends, creative and free spirited in that slightly crazy way that is common to retirees released from commitments with a new lease of life. We went our separate ways in the sunshine to the sound of crashing waves, feeling at one with the elements and each other, renewed and strengthened.

I reflected on my cycle ride home along the seafront, how the sea constantly regenerates, moves and gives life. Primeval and womblike, it evokes unconscious memories and thoughts. This whole kingdom of water; silky, shiny, soothing and beautiful in its summer glory, its different lights and hues, iridescent on the surface; often blue, green, beige, pink, lilac and silver-grey. A constant source of inspiration for my artist friends and my passion for photography and writing. Sometimes turbulent stormy squalls catch a swimmer out, as she suddenly finds herself swimming against strong waves, beating rain and lightning strikes. And other times, a mirror-like calm, a vista all the way across the channel to Wales, southerly to Devon and northerly to Bristol, with such an expanse of sky meeting the sea and merging as one. The simplicity of sitting by the lake, dreaming across the water and feeling at peace with the world, has become my go-to happy place for meditation throughout the winter months.

Born under the water sign of Scorpio, I have always had an affinity with water and all that it symbolises. Growing up in a Cornish fishing village and then living on the Somerset coast, I feel at home by the sea. During the summer months, it was inevitable I would take to wild swimming. In the lake, I feel soft and fluid, bending and rolling as sinuously as a mermaid, free from the gravity of land. I lie on my back, carried by the wind as clouds sail on high. I take oxygen from both air and water, like a fish through its gills. My warm flesh and blood and beating heart pulse with the power and might of the sea. The briny coolness washes up my spine, tingling and refreshing the brain, while vital minerals are absorbed through the skin. The movement takes me where it will; safely tethered to my tow float, I have no fears. I hear the ancient roar of the sea crashing against the causeway and feel part of the universe and cycle of life. We might be flooded again, who knows? One day, perhaps the oceans will once again cover the earth and life will exist only in water as it did at the very beginning of life on Earth. *The sea is a powerful force and nature will always have the last word.*

Shadows of the Cinnamon Apple Trees

Lois Elsden

On the paths of the yard the shadows of the cinnamon-apple trees are inky black. I look at the damned trees and silently ask them where in heaven's name are their cinnamon apples. They have been given the best and kindest attention, they have been nurtured, they have been given the required 10 + gallons (yes gallons) of water throughout the fruiting season. They should love my littoral location, apparently favouring coastal environs. They had blossomed as they should have, and although I could not detect any hint of the supposed delicate cinnamon scent of the pretty pink flowers, there were plenty of them. As there had been last year.

This year, in case the British insects weren't doing their pollination well enough, I'd employed a small water-colour paint brush as directed on a gardening basics web-site, to hand fertilise them. As with last year, the pretty blossoms had eventually browned and fallen off, leaving no proto-cinnamon applets.

I cast my malevolent gaze upon the wretched trees, baking in the searing heat of what is now a typical English summer. I sigh heavily. Well at least the small trees are pretty, and their dense leafage casts onyx shade, and I step down onto the path and wander over to sit in their pleasant shade. Nothing stirs, there is no sound, it's as if the world has turned itself off, stopped. The whole garden is still as marble. I shouldn't really care about the trees, accepting they are attractive, and despite not doing much fertilising, the bees and insects do love them, and in spring the pretty flowers are a-buzz with the sound of tiny wings.

I could have grown any fruit trees here, it was a stupid promise, a boast, to the then beloved, now departed, who adored cinnamon. I would not only make him cinnamon apple pies galore, and pasties, and turnovers, and crumbles, and cakes – but I would grow apples which would taste of his favoured spice. Apparently, the fruit themselves are a very pretty wine-red, with a yellow tinge and a creamy flesh. Well, I will never know because I'm pretty damned sure these fine trees will never be kind enough to honour me with any harvest.

When he departed, I was ready to chop the blasted trees down. I don't even like cinnamon, and I have more of a savoury taste than sweet. I actually went to the village hardware shop and looked though the garden tools section for a small axe, imagining a George Washington scenario, *"I did cut it with my hatchet,"* he had said, and I would say, although it was a cherry tree not a cinnamon apple tree he chopped down.

I sit in the deepest black shade out of the screaming sun. Why am I even bothered about the fruit? I don't like cinnamon, in fact I actively dislike cinnamon. I sit in the silent garden, and nothing moves, the world for a moment is petrified, turned to stone, as marble, on the paths of the yard the shadows of the cinnamon-apple trees are inky black.

Dressing Up

Brian Price

On the paths of the yard the shadows of the cinnamon-apple trees are inky black. The whole garden is still as marble. The heavy scent of eucalyptus drifts over the wall, blanketing the residual smell from the barbecue. Something flitters across the face of the moon and Sheila, motionless on the recliner, an empty glass beside her, wonders whether it's a bat or a nocturnal bird. A bat would be more appropriate, she thinks. It is Halloween, after all.

There is a rustle under the trees and a tall figure steps out. Clothed in black, it appears to be brandishing a scythe, like the one her husband keeps in the shed.

"Oh, Bruce," she giggles. "You didn't have to dress up. Halloween is for kids, and American ones, at that. We're too old for that sort of nonsense."

The figure pauses, as if puzzled, then comes nearer.

"I like the blue lights in your eyes, though," she continues. "I suppose they're LEDs. But where did you get the robes? I'm sure I didn't have any black cloth in my sewing cupboard."

"COME WITH ME," the figure intones, speaking as if his words were in capitals.

"Don't be silly, Bruce. If that's your idea of a romantic overture, I'm afraid you're backing the wrong wallaby. Off you go, and get me another drink. My glass has been empty for bloody ages."

Her husband calls out. "Fancy another G&T, Sheila?"

The voice came from behind her.

"SOD THIS FOR A LAUGH", the figure in front of her says, stomping off into the shadows. "I WILL BE BACK."

Poet's Retreat

Macaque

On the paths of the yard the shadows
Of the cinnamon-apple trees are inky black.
The whole garden is still as marble.

From the edge of the heat, waders warble
Out of sight, their throats slack
Like the wisteria hanging in rows

Along the south wall. The smell of bladder wrack
And the throaty sound of a thousand pebbles
Jostling under the rhythmic throes

Of the turning tide intrude, impose
Upon this still and silent haven the burble
Of the outside world, everything I want the knack

Of forgetting - the threatening tick of the clock I didn't unpack,
Memento mori of the endless jumble
Of commuting, commerce, chaos. I just want to repose,

Enjoy the garden, compose not decompose,
Wait in the shade for an apple to tumble,
Delight in the scent of cinnamon as it cracks.

Crime Story

A Peculiar Sighting

Brian Price

I was browsing idly through Facebook when I came across a dead man.

I don't normally look at people's stories. I don't need to see what people are eating for lunch, or what exotic holidays they're enjoying. But this one caught my eye. A bearded guy, in a pub garden in the sunshine, extolling the virtues of Theakston's Old Peculiar.

Sunlight glinted off the glass, and the dark beer it contained cast a shadow over the man's face. But when he moved the pint, his face was clear. Take away the beard, darken the grey hairs, and it was Derek Holmes. The Derek Holmes who I went to school with, who was best man at my wedding and who died in a car seven years ago. So, what the hell was he doing in the beer garden of the Jolly Ploughman, obviously thriving, and enjoying a pint of Yorkshire's 'lunatic broth'?

Now, I don't believe in ghosts, or zombies, or any of that supernatural bollocks. But seeing him there made me shiver. So, the first thing I did was take a screenshot of his face and compare it with some old photographs of the two of us. No doubt. It was Derek. So how could I explain this?

The name he was using, on Facebook, at least, was Paul Brickworth. I sent a friend request but it was declined. Surely, he would recognise my name and get in touch? We were best mates for years and we never fell out over anything. Apart from Sally Morpeth, I suppose, but that blew over when she married the local vicar.

How could I make contact? The video was only half an hour old, so I had an idea. I looked up the pub on the internet and found a phone number. I called them and asked if they could bring a bearded customer, currently in the beer garden, to the phone. The woman who answered clearly thought I was mad, but she complied and, a couple of minutes later, I heard a familiar voice on the phone.

"Paul Brickworth speaking."
"Derek. It's me. Steve Forrester."
There was a silence at the end of the line.
"Do I know you?"
"Well, we grew up together. You bloody well should."

"Sorry, mate. I don't know who you are. I've gotta go. My beer's getting warm."

"No. Hold on. What does the name Sally Morpeth mean to you?"

Silence.

"OK. If you're who you say you are, what poster did I have on my bedroom wall?"

I thought for a moment. There were several, but his favourite was a Dali print, *The Persistence of Memory*. When I told him this he relaxed.

"OK. Perhaps I owe you an explanation. Where are you?"

"Still in Kettering."

"Can you meet me at Leicester Forest services on the M1 tomorrow night, around ten? I'm not being overdramatic, but make sure you're not followed."

"OK," I said, "But what's with the spook stuff?"

"Never mind. I'll explain. See you."

He rang off.

I didn't know what to make of this crazy scenario. From a Yorkshire pub, and a Kettering semi, we seem to have been plunged into James Bond territory. Still, I resolved to meet him and would keep my eyes open, as instructed.

***

The services were quiet, with only a scattering of travellers taking advantage of the culinary treats on offer. Derek was in a corner, with his back to the wall, holding a cup of coffee that looked as though it had been made some time ago. His eyes flickered to and fro, sweeping the other customers, and he tensed when he saw me. As we shook hands, he relaxed a little, but continued to scan the area, presumably for threats.

"How are you mate?" I asked. "What on earth happened?"

"A long story," he replied, a hint of his former infectious grin passing fleetingly over his face. "Sit down and I'll tell you what I can. Are you sure you weren't followed?"

I nodded.

"OK. Well, everyone thought I had died when the car went over the cliff. Obviously, I didn't. The thing is, I'd got involved with a few dodgy blokes, and one of them was hassling me to look after some heroin and a gun. I didn't want to do that, but he was very persuasive. We met in my car, and he said my family would be hurt if I didn't do as I was told. He pulled out a knife so I hit him. Hard. I nearly threw up when I realised I'd killed him.

"OK, I could have argued self-defence, as he had the knife. Reasonable force and all that. But I was much more scared of his mates than the law. So, I decided to get rid of the body and fake my own death. I did the bloke's seat belt up, drove to Gravity Point and checked the tide was fully in. I opened the driver's door and pushed the car off the cliff, leaving my wallet and phone inside. The car floated for a bit, sank, and then the tide carried it away. I knew it would wash up somewhere, and they'd assume I'd been lost to the sea."

"Well, it worked. Everyone thought you were dead. What did you do then?"

"I'd grabbed a bundle of cash off the guy and taken his coat. My sister was on holiday for a couple of weeks, so I dossed at her place while my beard started to grow. I dyed my hair and, when I felt confident, I worked my way up to Yorkshire. I've been doing odd jobs, where people don't ask for references and NI numbers. I'm OK, though I suppose I'll have to re-emerge eventually. By then I hope the gang will have lost interest or been jailed."

"Why the Facebook post?"

"Well, I've always liked a pint and I got careless. I didn't think anyone would recognise me. But you did."

I nodded slowly. I knew what I had to do and I knew it would hurt both of us.

"There's a problem, Derek. Your passenger was still alive when the car hit the water. There was seawater in his lungs. You killed him and you can't claim self-defence. I'm sorry."

I stood up.

"After you 'died' I changed career. I joined the police as a mature entrant. I really hate doing this, but, Derek Holmes, I am arresting you on suspicion of manslaughter. You do not have to say anything but it may harm your defence..."

As I recited the caution, a look of utter betrayal crossed his face. He offered no resistance and just slumped in his chair, while I called for a police car to take him away. I know I took an oath to uphold the law, without fear or favour, but, just now, I really wished I'd never came across my old friend on sodding Facebook.

Crime View

Lois Elsden

We didn't know when we rented it that the cottage was called Crime View. The estate agent said it was Lake View and all the literature and papers we got said Lake View, but they were printed by the estate agent. I'd lived in Manchester for a while, but had not really travelled out of the city much and certainly hadn't been to, and in fact not even heard of, Crime Lake, nor the village of Odcott where the cottage was. When I say village, I guess most people would have the same image as we had, of a group of cottages and houses with maybe a church, maybe a shop, hopefully a pub. It was all very last minute which was why we hadn't done as much research as we should have, but even if we had, we wouldn't have learned much.

What we did know was that the cottage was available, it had what we needed, a bedroom for Jaffa and me, another for Frances and a tiny spare, all the usual, bathroom, kitchen, living room, space to park one car - yes, in an emergency it would do, and in fact, it may do very well. We had been unexpectedly let down on the place we had thought we were renting, AirBnB we muttered. Furious, anxious, philosophical, desperate we continued to pack because wherever we ended up staying, it had to be near enough Castleton where Jaffa had his new job, and Hathersage where Frances had hers. I was finishing my doctorate, so as long as I had a good internet connection I could be anywhere. What with the area being in the National Park and a famous tourist destination, and not that far from Sheffield, there wasn't - at least now when we desperately needed it, much accommodation.

So, when one of the estate agents we had rung/emailed/messaged/Facebooked got in touch offering this cottage in a small village we literally snatched at it and sent back a large deposit. As we began to tidy round, everything packed in the cars, we had time to think that actually, maybe this might be a more interesting option. Who didn't like the idea of living in a village? It seemed to have all we wanted and needed, the travel might be more awkward, and a bit further, Odcott was well and truly off the beaten track, but it looked over the interesting sounding Crime Lake, perhaps we had been lucky!

On the way, Jaffa looked up Crime Lake, and Wikipedia told us that it forms part of a country park and resulted from canal works in 1794... the name 'Crime' may have come from a local word for "meadow". Of course, we realised this was a different Crime Lake, near Oldham in a place called Daisy Nook. "Our" Crime Lake was in Derbyshire, and as far as we could find out, that was just its name and it wasn't associated with any particular crime. Crime may, like the Oldham lake, very well have just meant 'meadow by the lake'.

We drove up in tandem, Jaffa and me in our car, Frances following behind in hers and arrived, eventually, in the dark. We found the key in the key safe as promised, let ourselves in and unpacked everything as quickly as we could. The reason for our rushing? Jaffa and Frances both started work the following day. At one point we'd anticipated staying in a B & B, but fortunately here we were, in Crime View, with Crime Lake somewhere nearby.

We kipped in sleeping bags, too exhausted to make beds and with early starts the next day. The following morning was an equal rush, black coffee as we had no milk, hasty showers and thankfully, although the bathroom was tiny, the water was hot. Then grabbing their things, they left me, with a quick hug and my best wishes for them in their new jobs.

And I was alone in Crime View. I slumped in the small but comfortable window seat, with a coffee and a view of what might be a farmhouse, down to trees and the glitter of what might be Crime Lake. There was not much to do in the little cottage. It was furnished and all our things were in storage waiting for us to find a proper home of our own once we were more familiar with the area. Maybe I should start organising things and sort Jaffa and my clothes and belongings... but maybe I would do it later. Maybe now I would go and explore Odcott and go and have a look at Crime Lake.

***

It might be cold by the water, but in fact it was pretty cold *not* by the water. I had left the cottage and wandered up what you might call the main road. In fact little more than a lane which, after a cattle grid, petered out into a stony, rutted track. Our cottage, Crime View, was in the middle of a row of three; the one we'd passed as we arrived looked empty, although there were drawn curtains at the windows. Maybe a holiday home, uninhabited at this mid-autumn time of year. The one on the other side was actually boarded up...

so much for having friendly neighbours, we didn't have any neighbours!

Facing us across the narrow lane was the end wall of a barn, windowless. When I'd walked up past it I could see into what looked like a farmyard, empty apart from a station wagon and a tractor. No sign of life, although I did hear some sheep bleating. Heading in the other direction was the small heart of the village, a post office, not open today but would be tomorrow, a pub which looked very shut, and a few rows of cottages, similar to ours. There were a few cars parked, flowers on windowsills, bits and pieces in the small front gardens, a few tubs with fading plants – yes there were people about, just not out and about!

It didn't take me long to take in the sights of Odcott. The village comprised an interesting old church, squat and hunkered down and closed, beside a Georgian house next to it with name plate, 'The Vicarage'. A building which must have been a school, was now converted into a home next to a square building with 'Chapel' carved onto a stone plaque. Had this village ever been a thriving, lively place? Hard to imagine.

I walked back down the road we'd driven up last night, glad I'd put a thick jumper on under my fleece. I'd wound a scarf round me, but was sorry I'd not thought to bring a hat. It was mighty cold. There were gate posts in the dry-stone wall, no gate but a sign pointing down to the lake. It was a bumpy, stony track, but easy walking – downhill at least. I stopped and sat down on a wrought iron bench with worn wooden slats because there was a view! There was a spinney of near naked trees below me, and a wonderful range of hills in the distance. The sun suddenly appeared and cheered everything up. and looking further along the path I could see the sparkle of the lake. I left the bench and followed the way down the hill, thinking I'd be puffing and panting coming back up.

The sun might be showing, but it was pretty parky, and it seemed to get parkier as I descended. I stopped to read a noticeboard, and it was as if I was standing in the shade, so very cold now. I guess valley bottoms take a long time to warm up. The notice board explained that the jealous wife of the Crime village blacksmith had murdered her husband, drowning him in the lake. Periodically he emerges from the lake with a hammer and goes in search of her, seeking justice and revenge. That was the legend; more recently (for recent, take 1854), Hilda Thurston, wife of the vicar of Crime Chapel, had struck her husband Frederick with the oar of the rowing boat they were in and he too had drowned. Cheerful.

I looked round. There was absolutely no-one in sight, and apart from a single bleating which I presume came from a single sheep, there was no sound or sight of any life. Not so much as a tweet of a bird. I've lived in cities all my life, I'm super aware of any danger strangers may pose. Out here in the abandoned countryside, there were no strangers, in fact there were no people at all – the last person I'd seen apart from Jaffa and Frances was another motorist filling their car at the petrol station last night.

I set off again, walking as rapidly as I safely could down the stony path, trying to shake off the chill. There was a small plantation of scruffy fir trees, I couldn't tell what variety they were, in fact I couldn't even think of any varieties of fir trees. I guess I was thinking about things like this because, to be honest, this lonely and desolate place was a bit creepy. What an effete townie I am.

Stepping out from among the trees was like opening a freezer door. There was a scrubby area of grass and I followed the track through it and came to wooden fencing, beyond which was the lake. I'd seen it when I'd emerged from the fir trees, and instead of thinking, 'oooh! There's the lake,' excited and interested, I'd felt reluctant for some reason, but had forced myself to continue.

I can't say why I felt so strange. Maybe I was tired from the drive yesterday, from the suppressed anxiety about where we were going, a subdued feeling of regret at leaving overwhelming the excitement of a new adventure. I tried to rationalise my feelings of disquiet about it, a lake is only a body of water – and then I wished I hadn't thought '*body*' of water.

I pushed open the gate and shut it behind me, remembering some country code instruction on closing gates. The grass was even more sparse and gave way to rocks and pebbles and there was the grey, turgid water, lapping sluggishly. There was a bitter wind now. It had been cold in the village, and on the path down to the trees, but the terrible chill coming off Crime Lake was something else.

Water is dangerous, wherever there's water – canals, rivers, pools, ponds and lakes there are notices warning of the possible peril. But why would it be dangerous to me, standing a dozen yards from the edge? Did I imagine a dripping vicar armed with an oar, or a sodden blacksmith and his hammer emerging, bent on revenge?

I turned and ran, as if I'd conjured them by imagining them. I couldn't work the latch on the gate and was about to try to clamber over when it gave and I almost tumbled through. I didn't fail to close it properly, anything to delay whatever it was I imagined. I ran, stumbling, almost tumbling across the sparse grass towards the fir trees, which now seemed like spindly soldiers, waiting to defend me. I stopped when I got to the bottom of the stony path. I didn't look back although my skin crawled. I tried to summon enough energy to head back up the hill.

***

"So what have you been up to all day?" Jaffa asked, giving me a hug. He'd stopped at a Chinese on the way back from Castleton and picked up dinner for us.

"I've been sorting stuff out, putting away what I can."

"Been out exploring?" he asked, pulling off his coat. "It's lovely and warm in here, glad you've got the fire going."

"I just had a quick wander round the village," I replied. "It's been a quiet sort of day really." I gave him another hug. "But I'm glad to see you home!"

_Honesty

Macaque

The papers had been full of it to begin with; all the gory details. All the elements had been there – politics, heroism, murder, an incensed villain, a brave victim, a grieving family – the media had lapped it up, initially. Then there had been a closed courtroom for the long-delayed trial, followed by a notable silence. The world moved on. Perhaps you remember it, now; perhaps you don't. Just another news item that didn't really touch your own life.

Googling it today, the details of the trial are slim. All anyone could find now would be the politician's unquestionable account of the events. How, after months of simmering dissent, Michael Forbes, a young councillor, had stormed into Conservative MP Alastair Cordwell's office at 20:05 on the 13th November 2018 and attacked the terrified man with a well-maintained WWII bayonet. He had slashed at him without warning, cutting him on his forearms and cheek, and damaging the antique desk as the politician had scrambled over it to get away. Hearing the commotion, Mr Cordwell's aide, Trevor Fray, had rushed into the room and tackled Mr Forbes, sustaining two stab wounds to the chest, the first of which had been fatal. Mr Forbes had then fled the scene, removing the hard drive to the CCTV cameras on his way out. The shaken and bleeding MP had called for an ambulance, playing down his own injuries and commending the bravery of his PA, vowing to support his bereft family in the aftermath of the tragic attack. Mr Forbes had been arrested at his home at 21:30 that evening by armed police officers, but had put up no resistance, denying all charges of assault and murder. He is now serving life in HMP Manchester, formerly known as Strangeways.

A diligent search would uncover a leaked statement from the defendant that he had indeed entered Mr Cordwell's s office that night, angry about certain environmental issues that were being side-lined, but all he had done with the bayonet had been to pin his letter of resignation to the desk in as pointed a manner as he could. And why the bayonet? Apparently, it had been a congratulatory gift from the MP for 'cutting the mustard' a couple of years previously;

by returning the gift with the resignation, Mr Forbes was making a point of ending the friendship as well as the business relationship. Severing all ties, as it were.

So, what really happened? Does anybody know? Was the CCTV footage ever recovered? Why am I rambling on about it, and asking myself these rhetorical questions, like I'm narrating some dumbed down TV documentary? All good questions.

No, the footage was never recovered; Mr Forbes' house, car, garage and garden were all thoroughly searched. His journey home was pieced together from other footage obtained by the police, and no stops were made that could account for the disposal of the hard drive. But at least two people know the truth, probably three: Mr Cordwell, of course; his lawyer, most likely; and me. I know the truth.

You can call me H. Think of me like V in that film, V for Vendetta: I am no hero nor heroine, no hermaphrodite with a halo, more a helmsman, a haruspex, a harbinger hailing the holocaust, a hornblower raising hackles, heisting the hum-drum, hijacking hedonism, harbouring the hallowed, the halcyon, the heavenly. I am a hornswoggler highlighting heresy, heckling hubris, the hackneyed hallmark of a haggard society, halting the habitual hypnotism of the headlines that harness the hopeless, hapless, helpless herds hobbling head-on into the hotbed of hierarchical hullaballoo, hoodwinking hoodlums without histrionics, helping the hounded and unheeded, harnessing hope in this horrible, hectic, headlong helter-skelter. The mask I hide behind is a firewall. I am a heuristic hacker, a hactivist, if you will, henceforth and hereafter, H.

In the summer of 2018 I sat in a booth in a café in the centre of town, demonstrating a particular skill to a prospective client. I logged into the CCTV network of the café and recorded an MP4 montage of all the cameras on the network. Basic stuff, really, but the client was impressed. After the demonstration, however, I noticed another network with some encrypted shielding, and my curiosity bested me. After a minute's fingertip exploration with my keypad, I found myself staring down at a famous Tory politician. The cameras were mute, so there was no audio feed, but I was still struck by the potential of my accidental discovery. I copied what I had done with my laptop on a small tablet, connected it to a large HD drive and external battery pack, then set it to record at certain times of the day, and taped it under the seat of the booth.

Over the following couple of months, I would pop into the café and swap the drive and the chargers, and when I had some spare time, I would review the footage, hoping to see some shady-looking deals going down, bribes being taken, perhaps some heated arguments or evidence of drug use. I altered the recording times when I realised how late the politician stayed in the office, but much of what I recorded offered me nothing whatsoever of interest. By October, however, I had managed to capture an illicit affair. Even without sound, I had recorded solid proof of an extra-marital relationship between Mr Cordwell and Claire Fray, the wife of his aide. I had edited what I had collected into a two-minute video to upload to my anonymous streaming site, H_for_Honesty.co.uk, but before I got the chance the news story about the attack broke, and it seemed insensitive to expose the infidelity in the wake of the poor man's murder. And then came the detail about the missing CCTV footage, and how Mr Forbes was pleading his innocence contrary to all the circumstantial evidence. So, I returned to the café the next day, swapped the drives, and watched the events unfold.

The wide-angle lens is mounted above the door, opposite Mr Cordwell's antique desk. The MP sits behind the desk with some papers and a tumbler of whisky. He jumps as Mr Forbes strides into the room. Mr Forbes is hyped up, Mr Cordwell seems unconcerned after the initial intrusion, accustomed to confronting strong opinions. Mr Forbes raises the bayonet in his right hand, places a letter on the desk with his left, then stabs the blade through the letter and marches out of the office, leaving the bayonet planted firmly in the desktop. Still calm, Mr Cordwell takes the knife by the handle and wiggles it free; he sits back down and reads the letter. He swivels in his chair for a minute, contemplating, reading the letter, and turning the bayonet over in his hand. Then he reaches a decision. He stands up, pours and drains another tumbler of whisky; he comes round to the front of the desk and slashes it a couple of times, with equally as much vigour as Mr Forbes had used. Then he clambers across the desk, pushing the papers, lamp and decanter onto the floor. Without hesitation, he swipes the tip of the bayonet down his left cheek, checks for blood, then holds his left forearm across his chest and slashes at it a couple of times; he pauses, looking at the knife, then he sits and holds it clamped between his knees, and cuts the correct part of his right forearm. He stands again and presses the intercom button on the desk phone. He speaks, then walks round to the front of the desk and drops onto his knees, looking helpless. Mr Fray enters the room; takes in the scene before him; rushes to the stricken MP who holds out his left arm in a plea for help. As the aide kneels down in front of him, Mr Cordwell deals him the fatal stab wounds with his right arm, and pushes him backwards onto the floor. He pauses again, assessing, formulating. He kneels beside the dead man and places his hands over the wounds like a first responder, puts a finger to his jugular. He folds the corpse's fingers around the hilt of the bayonet, as if Mr Fray had been the one to remove the blade in panic. Then he leaves the room.

Switching to the outer office camera, I see him remove the hard drive, and, back to camera one, open the safe behind his desk and place the hard drive inside. He also finds the letter and its envelope from among the papers on the floor, and deposits them in the safe, too, before locking it. Now he makes the phone call to the emergency services before sitting on the floor with his back against the desk and cradling the dead PA in his arms, rehearsing a stricken look.

It's been four years. There was all the media attention; the investigation; Mr Forbes was remanded in custody without bail; Eventually there was the trial with its own limited coverage; and then the sentence, and Mr Cordwell bravely returned to regular duties, his scarred cheek always turned to the camera, never missing an opportunity to exploit the tragic events, nor to offer comfort to Mr Fray's grieving widow; some of which I also have on video. He thinks he has got away with it, or at least, covered it up. The perfect crime in every way. The people believe him; the people support him. Now it's time to upload the truth.

H

Doctor

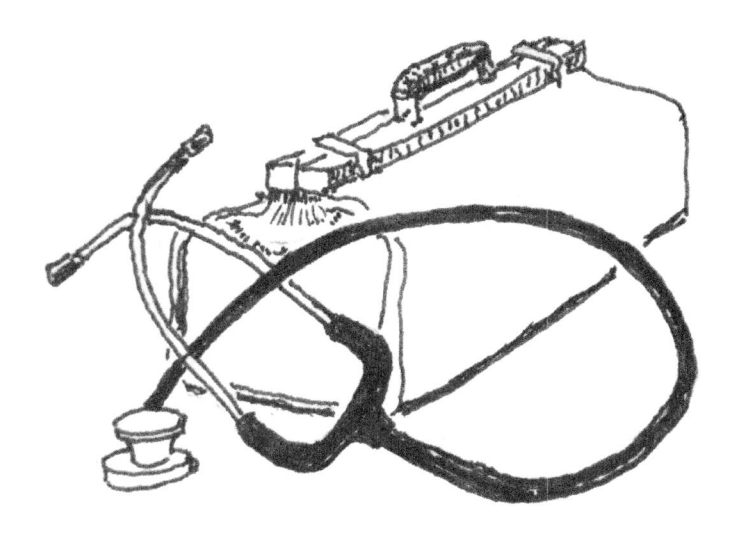

Doctor Chivers

Lois Elsden

I have almost come to believe that Dr Chivers never existed, that he was a figment of my imagination. However, I know he did exist - if he hadn't then I wouldn't be sitting right here, right now, coffee to hand, and with writing on my mind. All through my childhood I thought I would go to university, I dreamed of studying English, learning about literature and poetry, drama and writing. However, although I was born and lived in Cambridge, going to the University of Cambridge as my uncle had, was an impossible dream. Although, without being boastful or immodest, I knew I was clever enough. I also realised my temperament would let me down: lack of focus, a wandering mind, weird inspirations, misreading what was written and misunderstanding what I was supposed to do - in effect, unleashing my mental hobby-horse would not get me the results I needed. Thinking about it now, I'm pretty sure I would be diagnosed with ADD or ADHD if I was at school today.

At the grammar school I attended, I was forced to take Latin despite being spectacularly useless at it. In actual fact, getting into Uni to read English depended on having Latin. My ability to learn the subject was somewhat handicapped from the start - I was away from school for six weeks with glandular fever during the first term of studying the blasted subject. Our elderly Latin teacher was a dear old soul, but I just couldn't grasp the wretched language the way she taught it. I was further not helped by the school being ruled by a monster of a headmistress (think Miss Trunchbull without the physical violence but with plenty of other sorts of spite.) She would not let me give it up and do something else. Eighteen months before the exams, a brilliant new teacher, young and dynamic, took over. She was from New Zealand and she was wonderful and my grades improved dramatically as I began to grasp how the language worked. I was crushed when the headmistress refused to let me take the exam after all. No Latin, no reading English at uni. What a vindictive and nasty piece of work she was.

I changed school for my A-levels as we moved from the east of the country to the west, and if I'm honest, the new school I went to, and many of the teachers, although kindly, were useless. Despite working really hard, I only scraped through my A-level. In any case, I'd had precisely zero offers of a university place to study anything, in fact not even an interview to go to one. I could've gone to teacher training college in Matlock, in the depths of the Peak District, but I didn't want to be a teacher. Yes, I know, funny how fate conspires! I didn't get into journalism college, and in fact I didn't know what I was going to do. I realise now my parents must have been very understanding about my disappointment, and although no doubt worried which way my future would lead, they knew that I'd get a job and work hard at it. The summer holidays when everyone was getting ready to go away from home to study, I was back in Cambridge with relatives. I had a wonderful time and fell in love - which definitely took my mind off my academic future. I returned home and on a particularly sunny and lovely day the phone rang. Dad called me through - someone wished to speak to me. I couldn't imagine who it might be, but a hearty and cheerful voice greeted me and introduced himself as Dr Chivers of Manchester Polytechnic. He was inviting me to an interview for a place on a degree course in English, History and French. I felt as if I was standing in a brilliant shower of sparkling sunlight as I gabbled something, an acceptance of the invitation, and taking note of the time and date. No doubt my parents were as thrilled, delighted and excited as I was. This was in the days before there were many polytechnics, and in fact Manchester Polytechnic was brand new and I - if Dr Chivers accepted me, would be among the first students there! My granddad had been to London Polytechnic before the first war, he would've been so proud to think of me attempting to follow his example. I had been to Manchester once before, to the University on an A-level English course and had loved the city; the thought of going back was thrilling beyond words!

  I arrived at Piccadilly Station in Manchester with absolutely no idea where the Poly was and got in a taxi. The driver was similarly baffled and asked if I meant the Institute of Technology. *Polytechnic/technology, same thing, innit?* He drove me to the Institute of Science and Technology about a quarter of a mile from the station - I could have walked there quicker than it took to negotiate the traffic and find somewhere for him to stop. I climbed the steps of UMIST; there was barely anyone about because of course term hadn't started yet. I asked a porter and he asked his mate and they asked a passing person and no-one had heard of Manchester Polytechnic. "It's the Faculty of Commerce," I explained. "Oh, the College of Commerce!! Yes, go over that crossing, turn right and it's just there on the left, a big, grey tower block!" Within minutes, I was bounding up the steps in my brown, belted coat, a little gold orchid brooch on my lapel and an excited and nervous look on my face. I took the lift up to the eighth floor, along a narrow corridor with squeaky lino, and knocked on the door which had the name Dr Chivers inscribed. It was opened by a small man with a bald head and an exceedingly jolly face and sparkly glasses. It must have been the light reflecting off his lenses, but to me the sparkle spoke of magic and mystery. I must have been so keen and enthusiastic! I must have been so thrilled at being there, being interviewed by him, and maybe he hadn't got it in his heart to disappoint me, or maybe he saw something in me which convinced him I was worthy of a place. Maybe the Faculty of Commerce was so desperate for students that anyone who showed the slightest enthusiasm - and I would have been very enthusiastic and excited - would have had the offer shoved into their desperate hands. Whatever, Dr Chivers asked if I would like to join them on the following Monday! I was going to do a degree! I was going to be a student! I was going to Manchester!!

I can't now find any trace of Dr Chivers, in fact I can't find any trace of the College of Commerce, it may have become a Premier Inn. The polytechnic doesn't exist either – there's very little about Manchester Poly on-line. It has transmogrified into Manchester Metropolitan University the history of which barely mentions the Polytechnic, let alone the College of Commerce. But my life was changed there.

Thank you, Dr Chivers, I'm forever grateful, and I forgive you the comment you made on an essay of mine - describing it as 'journalistic bombast'. No doubt as usual I was carried away with over-enthusiasm and excitement and wrote a lot of nonsense about one of Napoleon's campaigns.

Doctor

Elizabeth Lawrence

    The hospital ward's entire aim was to be ready for the doctors' round by the end of the morning. Patients washed, hair combed, beds made with sharp envelope corners so that a long line of stiffness presented itself to the striding army of medics in their heavy leather shoes. Nurses were nimbler of foot with softer leather, an asset on night duty. Crisp white sheets were neatly folded over and tightly tucked under so that it was best to release arms in advance and slightly raise legs to avoid being clamped to the bed and lose all feeling in the limbs. The morning's medication had been meticulously administered and double-checked, and BPRs taken and charted (blood pressure, pulse and respiration – standard regular checks for all patients). All means of toileting having been expedited and bedpans washed in the sluice, a general air of freshness, antiseptic and efficiency prevailed.
    The team of serious-faced young doctors in white coats, led by a more mature consultant wearing an inscrutable expression and a three-piece tailored suit, strode onto the ward with great aplomb. Each patient was assessed in turn as the thin curtains were drawn around each bed with the illusion of soundproofing. In the background, nurses swiftly dealt with the wayward and confused, hurrying them along to the bathroom, pyjama bottoms falling down en route. Charts were studied, questions were asked of the duty nurse, and the patient's plight was pondered as if there were a team contest to provide the correct answer in the shortest time. An occasional command would bring a nurse scuttling to the rescue with a bedpan or kidney bowl.
    After the doctors' round, everyone relaxed as comforting clatter from the kitchen and warming aromas of gravy replaced TCP. The dinner ladies, usually large with bonhomie beaming from their good-natured faces and headscarves top-knotted neatly, would wheel an enormous mobile oven, doubling as a trolley, and dispense motherly comfort alongside old fashioned, wholesome food, always followed by a pudding with hot custard. Then more obs, naps and a hum of cosy domesticity as visitors arrived bearing flowers, grapes and chocolate, with the occasional bottle of whisky or Guinness secreted in a locker.

My mother wore her nurse's uniform with pride in the 1950s, belonging to a strict regime of starched aprons and stiff white hats. The hospital badge and belt buckle were polished and prominent. Wards were spotless and germ-free, cross-infection rare. Doctors were treated as nothing less than gods, but there was mutual respect for both professions and titles of Nurse and Doctor were always used as an address between the two.

I joined the nursing profession in the 1970s, on the back of these old school values and standards. The matron and ward sisters were highly respected and sometimes feared, for they could be dragons of harshness. But they ran a tight ship and compared with the sorry state of the NHS now, this was the golden age of quality healthcare accessible to all. There were, of course, a few exceptions in these halcyon days. During my nurse training, I did a stint of night duty on a geriatric ward. The duty night sister was rarely seen and the pupil nurse expected to run the ward until morning. I had some harrowing experiences which still haunt me today. Trying to single-handedly lift heavy patients who had soiled their bedding, whilst trying to clean around them, was distressing for both me and the patients, as they slipped, cold and confused. These people deserved better, and the ones who died in the night under such negligent circumstances will never be forgotten. But it was a privilege to care for people at this level, and some of the characters and connections of warmth, humour and stories, I will never forget.

Aside from hospitals, GPs back in the day were also easily accessed at surgeries and made regular house calls. Appointments were not even necessary in the 1960s; it was a matter of just showing up and being seen in an hour or so. As a young child, I dreaded being ill enough to warrant a house call. We didn't have to be seriously ill in those days, just a fever or earache would be sufficient concern for the doctor to call. Our village doctor usually called on his way home before his lunch break as he lived just round the corner. Consequently, my earache would often rage for hours before his arrival and I had to endure a morning of my mother running the house along the lines of a hospital ward. She had retained a reverence for doctors and admitting one into our house was an auspicious occasion. The whole house would be aired with open windows all morning, letting in the freshest of cool air, and then the vacuum cleaner vibrated in my feverish aching head. I would lie in a tidy bed with clean pyjamas and wait, feeling very tense. When the doctor finally arrived, with his big voice and even bigger body, I felt mine shrivel and tremble. I was scared of the large-statured person who would just walk in after a perfunctory knock at the door and proceed up the stairs. The black bag he carried held many frightening looking instruments. How I particularly hated the tongue pressers and the cold stethoscope on my thin chest, all the while dreading being prescribed foul tasting medicine. My mother addressed him as Doctor several times and I wondered if she might have curtsied. Despite the superior manner, I don't know how proficient the doctor might have been. I was poorly for several months and his only answer was to prescribe countless different antibiotics. I survived despite the treatment. A doctor was often known as 'the quack' and not always in fun. But our doctor was something of a celebrity in our small fishing village, and very handsome according to some of the women. He was the only one affluent enough to own a speed boat and attracted quite a gathering as he sported a wetsuit and took to the surf at the weekend.

In today's modern world, we are less in awe of our doctors and far more able to relate to them as equals, with respect for their profession, making for better communication and trust. Thankfully, there is now a healthy ratio of female to male doctors, equally happy wearing scrubs, crocs and ponytails. My GP looks like a mere slip of a girl, so friendly and kind and extremely confident, highly trained and brilliant, like many others. They may have some special qualities, but are by no means superhuman. It is incredibly difficult to make a doctor's appointment these days and extremely unlikely one would ever make a house call. But despite it all, I have faith in the dedication and expertise of those drawn to care for others.

Time for the Doctor

Brian Price

"Who?...No!...You're kidding me. Well, go and arrest him, then. I'll send a car."

Sergeant Whittaker put down the phone and looked around the squad room at the officers assembling for the night shift.

"We've got a result," he said, triumphantly. "PC McCoy's got eyes on our restaurant fraudster. She's picking him up now."

"How did she find him?" asked PC Piper.

"She was looking in a few restaurants along Mill Street, on her way back to the nick, when this waiter waved her over and whispered in her ear. Apparently, he works in two different restaurants – his father owns one and his uncle the other – and he recognised the bloke, despite his disguise. She went outside and phoned it in. Take a car, will you, Bill, and give her a hand? Someone's going to have a less exciting diet for a while."

Two weeks previously

An irritated Inspector Lambert stuck his head round the door as Sgt Whittaker started the shift briefing.

"Can I have a word, Jack?"

"Of course, boss."

"We've had a load of complaints from restaurants," began the inspector. "Someone's persistently stealing meals."

"But surely that goes on all the time?" a PC commented, "drunks eating and barging their way out without paying."

"Yes, but this is one bloke and he's doing it repeatedly. He's a bloody nuisance and the restaurants are demanding we do something about it. CID are up to their eyes, so it's down to uniforms keeping their eyes open. So, while you're out and about, look into restaurants from time to time and see if anything odd's going on."

"What does he do? How are we supposed to recognise him?"

"He books a table for early in the evening, under a false name. He eats, leaves his wallet on the table and tells the waiter he's going outside for a smoke while the dessert arrives. He's never seen again and the wallet is empty."

"Any fingerprints or DNA?"

"Don't be daft. We can't afford to pay for DNA testing in a case like this. And there are no prints on the wallet."

"What name does he use?"

"Several. Bill Hartley, Thomas Bakewell, Chris Exton, Jim Portlee, to name but four. He uses disguises and he's appeared as a silver-haired elderly gentleman, a younger man with a mass of brown curly hair, a short-haired man in a leather jacket and another older man, with white or grey curls. He's targeted The Punjab, Corleone's, Ming's and El Tacos among several others."

"Sorry to ask, guv," said PC Piper, "but why are we bothering with this when we've got fights to break up and real villains to nick?"

"Because the last restaurant he did, Las Tapas, is owned by the Deputy Mayor. So, keep your eyes open. Thanks, Sergeant. That's all."

The inspector left the room to murmurs of discontent and mutterings about priorities. PC McCoy said nothing but sat thoughtfully while the sergeant continued the briefing. There's something odd about this, she thought. There's a pattern, but I can't quite see it. It'll come to me.

For two weeks, uniformed patrols looked in at restaurants in the early evenings. No-one appeared to be acting suspiciously and the restaurant staff raised no concerns. But when Sarah McCoy looked in at the Old Mumbai, and the waiter called her over, she recognised the fraudster immediately. He was sitting at a table near the door, his wallet was next to his plate, his hair, obviously a wig, was blond and he was wearing a cricket jumper and a blazer with red edging. The penny dropped and she left the restaurant, reaching for her phone.

"So how come you recognised him, Sarah?" asked the inspector, after the suspect was brought into the station.

"He's some kind of deluded Doctor Who fan. Each time, he dresses up like one of the actors playing the Doctor. He runs the costume hire shop on the High Street so he has access to wigs, make-up and suitable clothes. This time he tried to make himself look like Peter Davison, the fifth Doctor."

"How do you know all this stuff?"

"My partner's a fan. We've got a mantlepiece full of Lego Doctor Whos and the cupboard's bursting with DVDs. Why would he bother doing this – pinching meals, I mean. His shop always seems busy so he can't be starving. Perhaps he thinks Doctor Who should get free meals – he never seems to eat. Do you think he'll serve time?"

"Lord knows. He's said nothing since you nicked him. He looks more like a psychiatric case than a criminal one. Maybe, if he agrees to compensate the restaurants, he'll get a suspended sentence or community service."

As the suspect was led to the cells, a flashing blue light from a police car outside shone through the window. The cell door made a grinding noise as it opened and, as it shut, the suspect spoke for the first time since his arrest.

"Where's my Tardis?"

When the Doctor Calls

Simon Phelps

My darling, homely, wife busied herself around me, tweaking my fine, long, embroidered waistcoat and tucking my linen shirt into the waistband of my breeches. She then knelt, and taking a cloth from her own waistband began burnishing my already glossy shoes and their chased silver buckles.

She paused and, looking up, said, "These are your finest clothes, husband. You're wearing these; for a dinner with the Merchant's Guild?"

My mind raced for an answer. There was no dinner. I needed an excuse to get my finest clothes out of the house. They had cost me a small fortune. "Ah, my dear, I wish to show off my success, and what better way than to arrive in all my finery."

"I suppose so, my husband, though I never thought you so vain."

I looked down at her fondly, feeling just a little tug at my heartstrings as I remembered this was the last day I would ever spend with her. Her dowry had staked my first merchant venture. That, in turn, had led to all the riches I have accrued to date.

She stood to straighten my lace cravat and turn my broad collar down over it. I looked down into her plain face and, on a sudden impulse, leant forward and kissed her on the lips. Her eyes widened in surprise, and blushing, she smiled.

"You so rarely kiss me these days," she said, smoothing her skirts, "I so love it when you do."

Momentarily lost for words I was saved by Mary, my wife's maidservant, coming through the door.

She bobbed a curtsey, "Ma'am, Kitty is getting worse. She's feverish now and has thrown up on the floor."

My wife sighed huffily, "Vomit is the politer word, Kitty. What do you expect me to do? Get Hal to clean it up."

"Hal has run for the doctor, Ma'am, as you told him to."

"You've sent for the physician for the ailments of a servant?" I scolded indignantly. Then, remembering that I wouldn't be paying, said, "Oh, never mind, perhaps it's for the best."

They bustled out of the room. I breathed deeply, relishing the relative quiet of being alone. I opened the window to let in some air. A mistake, the stinking miasma of the warming summer streets invaded my nostrils. I slammed the window shut. Thankfully my neighbour across the street was not in his chamber. Our upper stories are so close he likes to converse across the gap. Thank God for small mercies.

I was vaguely aware of a commotion downstairs as I lifted my wig from its glossy mahogany stand. I adjusted it gently, fearful of getting the powder on my clothes. One of my first tasks on arriving at my destination will be to employ a valet. Truth is: I am that vain.

My reverie was disturbed by a soft knocking on the door. I strode over and pulled it open. A most bizarre figure walked into the room. It stood before me under a wide brimmed hat. Its head was completely enclosed by a hood and its body draped in a long heavy cloak which reached to the floor. And, strangest of all, two owl-like glass eyeholes peered out from each side of a huge beaked mask. His hands were sheathed in thick leather gloves. He also carried a long stick. The whole ensemble reeked of lavender, cloves and other pungent spices.

I recoiled, though I had never seen this garb before, I knew its significance. "There is plague in the city?" I cried.

A muffled voice came from behind the mask, "Yes, sir, we are visited by one of the three arrows of God."

For a moment I was reminded of those dreadful Puritans who have so swiftly, thankfully, fallen out of favour. "Are the ships still sailing?" I blurted out.

"Ships sir?" came a puzzled reply, "I am talking of plague."

"Oh yes, sorry," I said. My ship, loaded with the entire contents of my warehouse, and all the gold I possess, waited for me and the rising tide,

Which reminded me, the tide was my deadline. I seated the wig upon my pate.

The muffled voice spoke again, "Sir, you need to listen to me. The City Authorities have empowered me to take all necessary measures to prevent contagion."

"Contagion, contagion," I expostulated, "You need look no further than the miasmas arising from our foul streets."

The voice got louder and indignant, "Sir, I am the physician. Putrefaction and contagion, I say. The streets will be fumigated but contagion must be stopped at source."

It dawned on me that this man was in my room for a reason. Usually he came and went, then sent his boy with the bill. "What do you mean, stopped at source?"

"When I discover a case of the plague my men will nail the house shut. You will be brought food which can be raised from the street in a basket into your upper floors."

"Me, why me?"

"I am trying to tell you. You have plague in your household, plague, sir, plague!"

I slumped onto the bed, dropped the wig and held my head in my hands. What was I to do? All my plans were set. It was now or it was never. My heart pounded, there was a rushing in my temples. I swear I was seeing red. I leapt up, grabbed the wig stand and thwacked the doctor right across his skull.

He slumped to the floor without a cry. I struck him again, then once more. On the last strike I felt a sickening crunch through the layer of thick felt. Tossing the wig stand on the bed I tore off the hat, the hood and the sinister mask, to see the familiar, gentle features of our family physician. The back of his head was a bloody mass.

Rocking back on my heels I heard feet on the stairs. I jumped up, ran to the door, to find Mary raising her hand to knock.

"What?" I snapped, "What do you want?"

She recoiled, "The mistress heard a thump. Is everything alright?"

I took a deep breath and answered much more gently. "Yes Mary, everything is fine. The doctor and I are just having a chat."

"Oh," she said, "Kitty is really ill. Can he make her better?"

"I'm sure he will. Never you mind. Now run along and leave me in peace. Tell your mistress, I, we, are not to be disturbed."

Shutting the door, I turned to face the doctor's corpse. What now? Suddenly I knew exactly what to do. I quickly disrobed the doctor, pulling off his huge cloak and tearing the mask and hood from his head. The hood stuck bloodily to his wig. I tugged it free. Bits of his bloody scalp came with it. I shuddered as I pulled the hood over my face and inhaled the sickening smell of the herbs and spices the beak was stuffed with. It was very hard to see through the eyeholes. I had the presence of mind to stuff my own wig down the front of the cloak. Then I pulled on the gloves. Picking up his cane I assessed myself. Hmmm, I was taller than the doctor had been. I bent my knees until the hem of the cloak swept the floor. I headed downstairs.

This was tricky. I couldn't see the treads and I was keeping my knees bent in case I was seen. I caught my toes on the cloak's hem and for a moment feared I was going to fly headlong down the stairs. I recovered myself with a gasp, my stick, by God's blessing, supported me. I sensed rather than saw someone near me as I reached the landing. Peering around through the thick glass I saw my wife's concerned face looming at me.

"Let me help you doctor, let me help."

I tried to wave her away but she grabbed my elbow and guided me to the next flight of stairs. I was trembling now as the excitement wore off and reality set in. I was a murderer.

"I'll go down in front of you," said my wife kindly, "put your hand on my shoulder and let me guide you."

As she helped me escape from her I felt a strange pang of guilt. I shook that uncomfortable feeling away, and, putting my hand on her soft shoulder, let her lead me down the last flight.

"You're trembling, doctor. Are you feeling alright? Would you like to stop for a glass of wine?"

I stopped myself from snapping at her. She's always asking stupid questions at the wrong time. Making some gruff noises and shaking my beak vigorously I pointed towards the door. Mary pulled it open. Daylight. I shuffled towards it in a painful half crouch. The door closed behind me.

I leant on the frame breathing hard, turning I became aware of three men and a sedan chair. Of course, the doctor's conveyance. One of the men waved a heavy looking lump hammer at me. I peered at him from the shadows of my mask to see him raise a very long nail into my view.

"Nail 'em in sir? Shall I nail 'em in?"

God, what to do? I wanted to tear the mask from my face, to suck in air, however foul, into my labouring lungs. Nail my wife in with the corpse of our doctor? It was the only thing to do. I nodded at the man, and grunted a subdued, "Yes," at him.

He gave me an odd look but proceeded to hammer in the first nail. I clambered into the sedan chair and tried to pull myself together. From the corner of my eye, I saw the round door catch of coiled black metal twisting frantically up and down as faint cries came from behind the thick wooden boards.

"Go, go," I called out to the sedan men. They lifted the chair then swayed from side to side.

"Whatever are you doing?" My voice must have been muffled enough for them to mistake me for the doctor.

"Where to, Sir, where to?"

"The docks, I need to get to the docks."

They shuffled uncertainly. I banged on the framework. "Do as I say. Go."

They headed off, slowly. I could have walked faster but to get out now would look suspicious. I held myself in, lulled by the gentle swaying as the chair swung in time to the even pace of the chairmen. I can't arrive at my ship dressed like this. No way would I be let on. They'd castoff as soon as I was seen for fear of being quarantined. I peered around trying to work out where we were. I recognised the façade of the infirmary as the steepness of the street increased. The front of the sedan chair was banging against the calves of the front bearer. I could hear his curses. Seized by a sudden inspiration I banged furiously on the ceiling of the sedan with the thick end of the stick.

"Stop here, put me down here. Put me down." The one place where no one would notice a physician is in the infirmary.

The chairmen muttered disrespectfully. Just loud enough to hear but not to make out the words. Churls. I was tempted to give them a piece of my mind when I recollected my fugitive status. Ignoring their outstretched palms, I pushed past them into the hospital.

Once inside I didn't feel so safe after all. The sedan chair men were shouting after me for their pay. In front of me, a corridor. My vision was so obscured I couldn't get my bearings. The glass panels seemed to have misted over. I blundered on, past some clerks, a trolley of evil looking bandages, another pair of doors, a ward. Running now, giving up all pretence of the physician's educated calm, I burst through a door at the end of the long room to find myself in dazzling sunshine. I cast down the stick, snatched off the gloves, shrugged the cloak off of my sweating body, then the hat, the hood. God I must look a sight. Something was missing. My wig. When I rummaged through the discarded clothing, fleas jumped from them. I took a moment to scorn the doctor's hygiene. I found the wig. The powder now in clumps. I stuck it on my head anyway. My tricorn, damn, that I had forgotten. Brushing myself down as best I could I felt a violent urge to be sick. I vomited, just missing the toes of my shoes. Apart from the foul taste in my mouth I have to admit I felt better. Sucking in some deep breaths I appraised my surroundings. I was in a narrow alley running behind the infirmary. Its steep slimy cobbles could only lead to one place, the quays.

I followed it down to emerge by the side of the Mariner's Church. I crossed the street and ducking under the bowsprits of the moored ships I dashed onward, through the bustling crowds of mariners and stevedores. I found my ship, providentially preparing to cast off. The pilot was stepping on board as I approached. I waved, shouted and ran swiftly to, and up, the gangplank.

The captain welcomed me aboard, "Your things have been stowed sir. You will be sharing my cabin as befits your status. Another few minutes, sir and we'd have left without you."

I thanked him with far more grace than my dishevelled self was feeling. I walked up to the stern deck and watched the filthy city dwindle into the distance. The first salt smells of the open sea refreshed my nostrils and lifted my spirits. I was free. I had escaped. A new life awaited. I felt a nip, I scratched, and felt another. A small price to pay. No one ever died from the bite of a flea.

Doctor in the House

Elizabeth Lawrence

Bernard sank his ample behind onto the cushioned bar stool and let out a gentle sigh as he and the stool merged into one. He was most partial to good 'real ale' and fortunately the landlord kept a fine brew at just the right temperature, poured to perfection into Bernard's own tankard kept behind the bar. He occupied this space for an hour or so most evenings, his only movement from the elbow, a hand to his glass and then raised to his lips.

A thatch of windswept hair and a ruddy complexion suggested he walked everywhere and paid little heed to his appearance. Thoughtful and bright-eyed behind thick lenses with heavy frames, his myopia gave an air of vulnerability. He listened to the comforting chatter and felt very much at home. He took everything in from his little bubble of reserve, and was in constant inner dialogue with himself, witty and ironic with many flashbacks to his intellectual past and wondering what his peers would make of the shower now in government. Bernard derived much from his hour in the local, escaping from the leader of the opposition and speaker of the house, who remained firmly indoors, glad of a chance to plump up the sofa cushions and throw out her husband's pile of newspapers and left-wing subversive, propaganda journals.

It was Christmastime, the fire was warm and the pub had outdone itself with the lights and lavish decorations. Bernard felt a spirit of welcome and friendship where everyone was accepted just for being themselves, unconditionally, like the ideal family he never had. The flickering orange flames and twinkling coloured lights seemed to shimmer and blur together and the whole room took on a warm glow. He felt himself entering another dimension, so relaxed, he nearly slid off his stool. 'Crikey, this beer is strong tonight!' he thought. Better have one more for the road.

Bernard was undemanding and unassuming, expecting nothing from anyone and gave little in return, presuming he had so little to give that would be of interest or value. But his face lit up if anyone spoke to him or included him in general conversation. They were amply rewarded by his quick wit and a gem to take home from his repertoire of stories. He had an original turn of phrase that would have everyone in fits of laughter, as he just sat there calmly as if it had nothing to do with him.

One of the regulars was frequently worse for wear and, when asked if he had witnessed the scene, Bernard would remark that he had been aware of the lady in question measuring herself against the carpet again. He was so cynical and unmoved by Christmas that no one took him seriously and teased him unmercifully about having to travel to his mother-in-law's on Christmas Day. Bernard just sat there, smiling, good natured, as if the world was very strange.

His nickname was Doc. Rumours were that he had been an Oxford Don. His accent was upper class with the quiet confidence and irreverence of the highly educated. He spoke slowly and thoughtfully in a croaky voice from a lifetime habit of woodbines, now finally given up after a few health scares. He never volunteered information or pushed himself forward in conversation, and so it was with great delight that another bar fly discovered that Bernard was indeed a Doctor of Philosophy.

"What's one o' them, then?" sounded a disappointed regular, "Always handy having a 'proper' doctor on the premises," he added.

"Well, I think philosophy benefits all of humankind and shows deep thinking on a humanitarian open-minded level, aside from economics and politics," replied one of the more bohemian drinkers, thoughtfully.

"Load of tosh!" declared another as Bernard sank further into his stool, his cheeks a little rosier with each pint of ale.

The young folk in the open public bar were in high spirits, making merry over a few more bevvies than usual. They appreciated the eclectic mix of local characters in the pub, such as old Bernard sitting in his usual corner; he provided stability, continuity and a contrast to their chaotic lives.

It was Christmas Eve and drinkers were starting to head home. Some of the men shook his hand as they left, wishing him a "Merry Christmas," and the women who held a soft spot for the gentle man took the liberty of calling him Bernie with a peck on the cheek. He beamed from ear to ear and truly thought Christmas had arrived early.

He knew he should be getting home to help the leader of the opposition with the inevitable last-minute preparations, but it felt so peaceful in the pub. Bernard sank even lower on his stool and quietly slipped to the floor, unnoticed until a crowd on the way out nearly stepped on him.

"Yikes, what's happened to Bernard! Is he alright?"

"Stand back! He's passed out!"

The landlord shouted for someone to run for the defibrillator and call an ambulance, but he soon realised that Bernard had died, peacefully, judging from his lingering smile.

"Is there a doctor in the house? Shouldn't we call a doctor?"

"Bernard was our doctor and the only one we needed. He will be sorely missed."

Wrecking Ball

Macaque

I picked up one of those lifestyle magazines from the square table in the corner of the waiting room, and feigned nonchalance flicking through it. Some of the pages had been removed for recipes or hairstyles or advice on relationships or maquillage, and I found myself reading half an interview with an author whose name and picture were probably now pinned to a cork board, face down. The only clue to their identity were the initials H.M. The top of the remaining page began mid-sentence:
'interview where you talked about that very briefly. As I remember, you were rather cryptic about how it all came to an end. Would you care to elaborate for our readers?
H.M: (Gives a wry chuckle) The ghost of Sid James.
Int: Yes, that's what you said before and I was intrigued. Was that figurative? Do you believe in ghosts?
H.M: Oh, I absolutely do, yes. I think any writer would tell you that the Earth holds memories of the past, and sensitive souls sometimes come across them.
Int: That's interesting. But how does it relate to the band? That wasn't your name?
H.M: No, we ended up as Wrecking Ball, having started out as Oedipus Wrecks. We all lived in a condemned terrace, the buildings on either side had already been gutted, and so we used to rehearse undisturbed, and have the best student parties where we would play in the lounge or the front bedroom, and the police were rarely ever called. Then we played the Union bar and developed quite a following. We changed our name to Wrecking Ball when we decided to play outside of the university – this was the North East, a very working-class town, and we didn't want an esoteric name that labelled us as poncey students, you know? So we got regular gigs at McCann's, Bourbon Street, The Royalty and a few other places, and we were popular.
Int: And were these original songs you were playing? Did you record an album or any demos?
H.M: We were talking to a local businessman who approached us after a gig one night. We had about enough material for an album, and he was prepared to pay for a studio session and a few hundred CDs; but when nobody knows you on the pub circuit,

you've got to keep the regulars happy with songs they know, and we played some classics. Our signature tune was Doctor Doctor by UFO. It has a lovely lead guitar intro, and we used to extend it; it was a way for me to show off a little, and it gave Johnny a moment to get a drink or chat to a girl, and Robin used to roll a cigarette. We used to play our own stuff at the Union bar, but only a couple would make it onto the pub sets.

Int: So, what went wrong? It sounds like you were all set to make it happen.

H.M: At the end of our final year, there was a Battle of the Bands competition, a chance for us to showcase our own material on a much bigger scale, maybe even get a legitimate recording deal. We had no trouble getting to the final, along with a band from Newcastle called Force 10. I knew their guitarist a little because he worked in a music shop I used to go to when I could. He had a genuine Gibson Les Paul and an Ibanez that I would have killed for, but then he did work in a guitar shop, he wasn't an impoverished student like I was. He seemed like a decent guy, but there was a bit of rivalry between our two bands. We were from different sides of the Tyne, for a start. Force 10's bass player was their driving force. He was about six foot three and wore a black cowboy hat and trench coat with his long black hair, and people used to call him The Undertaker after the TV wrestler at the time. I think he got a real kick out of this association, and he certainly had the ego of an American wrestling star. For my own part, I thought it was his ego problem that stopped them being as tight a band, both musically and socially, as we were, and so I was really confident that we were going to win, even though they were more established and experienced.

The final was held in the Sunderland Empire, a huge venue by our standards, and quite famous in its own right.

Int: The theatre where Sid James died on stage, is that right?

H.M: Yes, that's true, and it's something you learn very quickly when you visit the town; people still talk about it for some reason, it's like Stratford and Shakespeare.

Int: So, how did the contest go?

H.M: The first round went well, so well in fact that it's a little bit hazy. We were all hyped up, and we'd all had a few drinks, I don't think we ever played completely sober, and, well, there's a certain euphoria that you get when you perform, when everything goes right, you know? When the audience react to something that you have created, that you have written and performed, when you hit every note perfectly and the whole band are in time, linked by the same euphoria – it's as powerful as any narcotic in the world. And we were on top of the world that night, it was a real blast.

Now, something had been going on backstage of which I hadn't really been aware. Apparently, The Undertaker had undertaken to move in on Johnny's girlfriend. With all the excitement and the rivalry and the close quarters backstage, a powder keg situation began to develop, and I should have been more aware, I should have tried to diffuse it.

We were waiting in the wings at the end of Force 10's final set. Each band entered Stage Right and exited Stage Left, it was all well organised. As Force 10 lapped up their applause, I don't know if Johnny saw something between the bass player and his girl, but suddenly he shouted across the stage, "Hey, Hulk Hogan!" Now, as I say, I wasn't really aware of all that had transpired before that, but the one thing you didn't do was make fun of this guy's Undertaker persona. He strode across the stage, thrust his bass at one of the coordinators, and laid Johnny out with one huge right hook, then he pushed past us all before we could register what had happened. Johnny came round after a few seconds, but his nose was broken, and there was no way he could sing.

The stage was made ready, the drum kit and pedal boards were all in place, the audience were eager for our final performance, and we had no singer. When Force 10's singer heard what had happened, he gallantly came over and offered his services. He came up to me and said, "Look, I feel terrible about this. I don't know your songs, but if you want to do a cover with me, you can at least finish the competition." I asked him if he knew Doctor Doctor, and he said he did, so I told him to talk to Mark, our bassist, and he would explain the intro that we did, and I went and plugged in. The crowd erupted as I came into view, and I knew I had to fill in a bit and build their enthusiasm even more while the band sorted themselves out.

"Alright," I shouted, "who wants to make some racket?" There was a roar in response. I stamped on my pedal board and played a pentatonic riff, then gestured with my arm to the crowd. ROAR! Another riff with a screaming harmonic; ROAR! A descending blues scale right down to open E; ROAR. A demented trill using the whammy bar, another hungry roar. Robin got behind the drums, and Mark plugged his bass in, and I opened the wah-wah peddle slightly for that Michael Schenker tone, and started our gradual intro to the UFO song, backed by sustained bass notes and atmospheric cymbals. It was all sounding great, and the crowd were into it as I stepped right to the edge of the stage and began the song's proper introduction. The drums came in behind me, and the lights blazed. There was another roar from the crowd as the singer emerged from the wings, growing in fervour as the Force 10 fans recognised him. We began the cantering rhythm that led to the start of the vocals, that first chorus of 'Doctor, doctor, plee-ease'. I was just floating, I was so hyped up; I looked over at the singer, and he raised the mic and came in with "Doctor, doctor, give me the news, I've got a bad case of loving you." An entirely different Doctor Doctor song by Robert Palmer. It's hard to say just who faltered first, but within seconds we petered out to an ugly hubbub of laughter and jeering from the audience. And at that moment I heard it, that throaty, Cockney, ah-hah-hah-ha!

Int: You heard Sid James' laugh on stage?

H.M: Yes. And that just seemed to seal it, you know? I'm sure we could have put that one incident behind us and carried on with our plans to record and see where it might take us after uni, but we never played together again. I moved down South after graduation, got my job in the library and started writing, and that's that. All best forgotten about, really.

Int: Oh, I don't know about that; I think it would make a great story. Thank you for finally sharing it with our readers. It has been a real pleasure to meet you today ahead of the launch of the new novel; and dare I say, "Carry on Writing!"'

I glance up nervously, distracted by some activity at the reception desk. Time to face the music myself.

Rope

Ruth

Fenja Hill

On July 13th 1955, Ruth Ellis was hanged at HMP Holloway, after being found guilty of the murder of her lover.

He's drunk again. She backs away, making a fuss of putting the kettle on and looking for cups and spoons, but now he's behind her, arms snaking round her body to cup her breasts. He always wants her when he's been drinking, oblivious to her own needs. Right now, all she wants is peace. She's exhausted from work, and has had enough of men pawing at her. It would be so good to come home to someone who cared for her, loved her, wanted to make her happy.

She doesn't pull away though. She still bears the bruises on her body and in her heart, from the last time she did that. Instead, she turns in his arms and kisses him, whispering that he should go upstairs and that she will follow him in a moment.

She will never know what was wrong with her response, but as she flies backwards across the room, the imprint of his fingers already forming bruises on her face that she will struggle to hide with make-up tomorrow, she can see exactly how the rest of the night will go. And she is right.

In the morning, he is sweet and loving, and she plays along until he leaves. He will spend the day with friends at the racetrack and, if she's lucky, he will go home with them and stay overnight. She will have the afternoon to herself, and perhaps, after work this evening, she will come back to an empty house and a few hours of peace.

Not for the first time, she asks herself why she stays, and she struggles to find a response. When they met, he was dashing, exciting, and he doted on her. He took her dancing in the rare evenings when she wasn't working, and he hung around at the club when she *was* working, glaring at the men with whom she flirted and danced. Their first argument had been about exactly that. He called her a slut and she had pointed out that, when he went to a nightclub, he flirted with all the dancers and waitresses and expected them to respond to his advances. What, she asked, was the difference? Unable to justify himself, he had resorted to slapping her hard, and had immediately apologised and promised that it wouldn't happen again. It was just that he loved her so much and couldn't help being jealous.

The pattern was established.

She leaves her bed, washes and dresses, and stands at the window, cigarette in hand, watching the world go by. She could go and see Desmond; he was always happy to see her, but they both knew that it was David she loved, and it was unfair to string Desmond along. She went to him because he was kind to her, gentle in a way that David no longer was. She had even moved in with Desmond for a while, in an attempt to make David see what he was missing, but that backfired badly. She knows he started seeing someone else during that time and, even now, she suspects that that affair hasn't ended.

Two days pass, and she hasn't seen David. She's tried telephoning his friends, but they say they haven't seen him. She can hear laughter and singing in the background. She's convinced that he's there, with that woman. In desperation, she telephones Desmond and he comes straight round. She cries on his shoulder, sobbing that she wishes she were dead, and then that she wishes David were dead. She's already dead inside, she says. Desmond wants to make her feel better. He is always so sweet and loving. He goes out to his motor car and returns with a small bundle, wrapped in a scarf. He hands it to her, kisses her gently on the forehead, and leaves.

That night at work, she can think of nothing except the gun. She has never seen one before, except at the cinema. It's bigger that she would have imagined, and heavier. Desmond told her it was loaded with six bullets. She has left it lying on the Formica table in the kitchen, in full view; not that there's anyone there to see it. What if David comes back and sees it? What will he think? What if she goes home tonight and he shoots her dead? At least then this will all be over. She places her hand on her stomach, exactly where his fist landed just a few weeks ago, and holds back tears as she thinks of the tiny person who never had a chance; murdered before it was even alive.

She dances and flirts and thinks about the gun. She gets through the night, and heads home in the early hours, but she doesn't go to bed. She sits in the kitchen, looking at the gun. Perhaps she will find David and shoot herself in front of him. For a while she thinks this is a good idea, it will teach him a lesson, make him see how unhappy she is. Then she thinks she's being stupid;

she doesn't want to be dead; she wants to be happy. The sun rises and the day passes. Ruth hasn't moved from the kitchen table.

At 7.30, she still hasn't slept. She takes a bath and gets dressed. She stands in front of the mirror and realises she is wearing street clothes and not evening clothes. It's clear that she is not going to go to work, although she has no recollection of making that decision.

She moves to the hall, and stands looking at the telephone. Eventually she lifts the receiver and dials the number of David's friend in Hampstead; she knows it off by heart. A woman answers, and she asks for David. The woman giggles and says he's very busy, then she hangs up the phone.

It's not easy for a woman on her own to find a cab in this area after nine at night, but eventually she persuades one to stop, and she hands him a slip of paper, on which she has written the address; she is afraid that, if she speaks, she will break down. There must be something in her eyes, or perhaps it's the way she's clutching her handbag to her, or the lack of a coat or jacket in the chill of the night that makes the driver nervous. He insists she pay him now, and she complies.

As the cab pulls to a halt, Ruth briefly considers asking the driver to turn around and take her home. She has come this far though, so instead, she steps out of the car and thanks him; the car is moving even as she slams the door. The driver can't wait to get away from her. Later, he will have stories to tell.

She stands watching the front door of the Hampstead house. Her feet are unwilling to carry her forward, but then she sees that there is, after all, no need. David steps through the doorway of a nearby tobacconist shop, cigarettes in one hand and the lighter she gave him for his birthday in the other. She sees him just as he sees her, and it's only now that she understands why she came. She reaches into her handbag for the gun, raises it and points it at him. He's only a few feet away and she sees his expression clearly. He's laughing; he doesn't think she will do it. So, she does. She fires the gun once and he falls to the ground. Not laughing now. But not dead either. He looks puzzled, peering down at the blood on his shirt. She moves towards him.

This close, she can smell the whisky on his breath. It occurs to her now that he was probably drunk; that's why he laughed. She stands over him and fires the remaining bullets into his body.

She should be feeling something; after all, she loves this man and she has killed him. The gun feels heavier now that it's empty. Strange. And then, a nice man is taking the gun from her hand and telling her that he's a policeman (but where's his uniform?) and he is arresting her. That's good. Someone else can deal with the clearing up. Someone else can do the thinking for a while.

They make her go to court of course, which is only right because she killed someone. They ask her lots of questions but she doesn't see the point of answering because after all, she killed someone. They all know she killed someone, so what are they wasting their time for? If you kill someone, you have to die too, it's only fair. And she's so tired, she just wants it to be over.

They tell her that people are writing to the court, some even standing outside the prison, making a fuss. Lots of people don't want her hanged. But then what? It's a life for a life, and they should know that.

And soon it will be over. They brought her a glass of brandy this morning and now Mr Pierrepoint stands before her, adjusting the rope, and she smiles her thanks.

An Unintended Consequence

Brian Price

The exploding phone box wasn't my fault. Honestly, I had no idea they were going to do that when I provided the chemicals. It was just my bad luck that I got roped into it.

You see, I was a sort of broker. There were several of us who did home chemistry experiments, some of them perfectly legal and some less so, but ordering small quantities of chemicals could be tricky and more expensive. So, I would put in an order, to this supplier in East London, and divide up the purchases among my friends, weighing out their portions on a chemical balance if need be. I didn't ask what they wanted the chemicals for, but perhaps I should have carried out what's now called due diligence, and probed.

Potassium chlorate was one of the substances involved. It's now illegal to possess it without a licence, under counter-terrorism legislation, incidentally. Quite a few of us used it to make fireworks and the like, so I would have assumed that was what it was wanted for. The other chemical had uses as a solvent but, combined with the chlorate, it formed a powerful explosive. Making the material for the detonator was relatively straightforward, if you didn't breathe in the fumes too much, and you could buy Jetex fuse, for toy rocket motors, easily. You could use thin rope or string, soaked in something flammable, as a fuse, but the bought stuff was more reliable. So that was the package they used to build a small bomb.

I first heard that something had happened when a late news bulletin on (the relatively new) Radio One reported an explosion in South London. I found out a lot more at school the following day. The three culprits, I'll call them B, D and G, had been seen in the vicinity of the box after the explosion, which had broken every pane of glass apart from the one proclaiming that 'Persons damaging this telephone box will be prosecuted.' It was close to where one of them lived - the phrase about not doing something on your own doorstep springs to mind. Also, 'D' had his arm in a sling and was easily recognised by neighbours.

Needless to say, they were quickly arrested and charged. The school was obviously concerned. Not only was the whole enterprise extremely stupid, and could have cost someone their life; the school had its reputation to think about. All three were interviewed by the Head and they told him where they got the chemicals. Although I had nothing to do with the explosion itself, I was prevented from attending science lessons for weeks, as were B, D and G, in case we learned about explosives there, which was absolute nonsense. This included biology, and I completely missed out on the metamorphosis of the frog – sinister stuff indeed!

The culprits were fined, put on probation and had to pay towards the cost of repairing the phone box. No-one took any action against me, and we were all able to return to our O-level science lessons after the court case. I was instructed by the Head to end my home chemistry experiments, unless the chemistry teacher approved them in advance, so I stopped and sold my chemicals and equipment to the school. It didn't curb my enthusiasm for the subject, though, and I went on to study chemistry at university.

Those were the relatively innocent days of the late sixties. Poisons, of course, were controlled, as were explosive substances like TNT. But you could still buy ingredients to make your own fireworks and so on – sodium chlorate weedkiller, now banned, was available in chemists and gardening shops. B, D and G got off fairly lightly. If they had done the same idiotic prank a few years later, when the IRA was active in London, they would have ended up at Paddington Green police station having seven bells kicked out of them by the anti-terrorist group. They would also probably have completed their education in Borstal instead of the grammar school.

Now, we live in more dangerous times. Fortunately, the ingredients for explosive mixtures are much more tightly controlled, and vendors have to report suspicious purchases of some less controlled substances such as acetone. It is also fortunate that the culprits were unaware of the, rather unstable, explosive of choice now used by many terrorists. For, if you're stupid enough to blow up a phone box just round the corner, while being easily recognised, you are clearly quite capable of blowing yourself up while making TATP.

Rope

Elizabeth Lawrence

My mother hated rope.

"The Pharaoh wants to rope us all in, tether us together, beat us with a slungshot knotted with stone, until we have built his new empire and literally worked ourselves into the ground. He will not give us so much as an inch of rope for ourselves," she would say. "We are prisoners in our slavery."

She spoke with bitterness; my elderly father was forced to make bricks and build temples each day until he collapsed from thirst and exhaustion. He was thrashed and the slungshot struck him on the temple causing instant death, which in hindsight, my mother thought a blessing. "A man of his age being forced to work like an ox in the fields!" she wailed. He suffers no more.

Ropes were once versatile, useful features of our lives, she often mused. We would make them thick and strong, weaving our natural grass fibres and woody stalks so they would last. As children we played games of line-skipping, chanting and jumping under a long cracking rope as it whipped the ground. Oh! how we loved tug-of-war! We were a strong tribe, healthy and long-living. The Pharaoh saw a threat that we would form an army and rise against him. But why would we have wanted to fight when we had fertile land in which to live and prosper with the gift of the Nile, life-giving, cleansing and abundant, enabling us to voyage and sell our wares. Our once revered governor, Joseph, had been long forgotten and our people were seen as an unwelcome scourge.

The situation became deadly and threatening several moons ago when King Rameses decreed that all Hebrew male born babies should be killed. Our much-loved and dutiful midwives were ordered to kill all male babies at birth. Women in labour stopped sending for midwives, unless having previously gained their trust. They would give birth in secret, in long agonising hours often ending in the death of the baby and mother. Our infant mortality rate soared and I would try not to look as the newborns were thrown dead or alive into the square for the vultures to devour. The good midwives, God-fearing and dutiful, reported back to Pharaoh that the strong Hebrew women were giving birth before they could get there. All women became sad and fearful, there were no more smiles, joy or chatter and many secrets were kept. Women covered their pregnant swollen bellies and tried to hide their babies, but the soldiers would come at night and murder the innocent young. We were terrified.

We had a new baby brother at a time when my mother thought she was past childbearing age. He had no name, he was just 'baby'; my mother's attempt to resist bonding with her child, knowing he could be taken at any time. We felt from the beginning that baby was special, with his calm and gentle qualities. He demanded nothing and even when hungry would soothe himself with our little homemade pacifiers. We would still come and scoop him up, singing. He was our joy and gift from God. But of course, our family could not stay as it was.

"Miriam, Miriam!" I heard my mother cry, "come hide your baby brother, the soldiers are coming!"

I hurriedly put our rehearsed plan into action and wrapped baby firmly in linen so he would feel secure and gave him a pacifier of cloth dipped in honey. I rocked him and hummed gently until he fell asleep and then slid him into a panel between the two walls of our house, which were thick and almost sound proof. We gave the impression of having been working hard for hours on our patch of land, digging and planting as if we had no baby to care for. The soldiers roughly barged passed us and rampaged through our ordered house. Satisfied there was no sign of a baby, they spat in our direction and rode away.

My mother, visibly shaken, had to sit down a while on a stone to recover. "Miriam," she said, "our baby is becoming too big to hide. We must give him to the river and trust God to find a home for him. The river is our giver of life and will find a way for our baby. All of you are grown now and my work is done on this earth."

I felt alarm, not so much at my mother's suggestion but at her resigned tone. We scurried around making a basket of papyrus grass and mud, coated with tar to waterproof and float on the water. She fetched a long piece of rope, almost in a trance. I made preparations for an ostensible foraging expedition along the river. Now was a good time to set off as the soldiers would be at lunch eating or sleeping. I turned to my mother and I had not the heart to prise our baby from her bosom where she clasped him, inhaling the sweet baby scent from his silky head. She stroked his plump brown limbs and answered his contented gurgles with soft coos of her own. As they gazed at each other in adoration, I had no choice.

"Now, Mother!" I urged. "There is no more time," I added more softly, taking baby from her. I gently placed him in the basket and he settled in with only a momentary look of surprise from his soft brown eyes. We smiled and pinched his chubby cheeks. It was time to leave. As we walked, he was very content with his pacifier and enjoyed the swaying motion of the basket, looking over our shoulders intermittently and scanning the horizon.

It was a beautiful still day, almost ethereal with a pale blue mist rising from the Nile. We could hear melodious singing and splashing coming from the reeds, hastening us to crouch down with the basket. We saw the beautiful young women with glossy black hair shimmering in the sunlight, their opalescently opaque silky gowns giving them the appearance of water nymphs. My mother and I gave each other a glance of tacit understanding and reassurance, feeling this gentle spectacle before us could only be one of kindness. We secured our rope to the basket and, barely able to comprehend what we were doing, cast baby and basket into the waters. He was sleeping peacefully, unaware that he had been tossed into the mercy of the Nile. With our rope, we guided him slowly on the gentle flood tide and the basket gradually made its way downstream towards the palace in the direction of Cairo. I think my mother would have let herself be dragged under by the water and drowned, such a strong hold had she on the rope. Taking the rope from my mother's hands and throwing it into the water, I felt like a cruel midwife cutting the umbilical cord prematurely. My mother collapsed in my arms stifling sobs, as I led her to safety. I felt more fear for my mother than for my baby brother.

Our apprehension was eventually broken by sudden shrieks of delight and excitement as the young women wondered what they had found in the reeds. We hid and watched. The one we recognised as Pharaoh's daughter, the Princess Bithiah, pulled baby's basket onto the bank and tenderly uncovered his face, still sucking on the pacifier. Obviously enchanted, she lifted the plump little bundle placing him next to her heart with his head in the curve of her shoulder. He gave a little whimper.

"Why! He must surely need milk and is too young to be away from his mother!" the princess cried in some distress.

"I must find a wet nurse for this baby. It is providence that I should find this Hebrew child and care for him. My father need never know his origins, just that he was sent by God to me."

Leaving my mother with a finger of hush against my lips, I approached the princess with a cheerful "Humble pardons, your majesty," as she turned to face me, somewhat surprised. "I could not help overhearing that you are in need of a wet nurse? I know of a woman with plentiful milk who has just lost her child."

"Then bring her to me, my loyal subject," said the princess, "and we shall set up an employment contract."

After an interval of twenty minutes, I introduced my mother to the princess who was delighted at the prospect of a secure foster home for her new found baby and promised protection from the soldiers throughout his childhood. She named him Moses, a Hebrew name for 'pulling out of water'.

Moses' infancy was spent with his birth family in their home with regular visits to the palace and Princess Bithiah. He was grounded in Hebrew ways and traditions and never forgot who he was or the sufferings of his people. Growing up in the palace gave him status and recognition amongst all people. One day, he led a mass exodus of all his people from Egypt to the Promised Land where they lived the rest of their days in fullness and peace.

Down by the River

Macaque

Jordy

Rhope's dead.

Leeza

We're gonna tell all bout what happened to Rhope and all our part in what happened after, just like John said we should. That way there be no doubts in no-one's mind at all. That's what John said, anyway. Else people might be wondering and putting voices to them thoughts, and making things go bad for us.

Art

My name is Arthur, and I'm the eldest. After me comes Thorn; he was supposed to be Thomas but they wrote it as Thornas on the certificate, so now we just call him Thorn. Leeza comes next, and Jordy is the youngest at six. I'm fifteen, and I've had the most schooling, so it should be my job to write this whole thing down and explain it. By rights that should be my job, like it's my job to lock up at night and clean the rifle and all. But John says we should each write what we know about the matter, each in our own words. So that's how we'll do it.

Thorn

John knows we had nothing to do with any of it, not until it happened, least. Not before then, just after. But now we gotta tell other folks cos they all be asking, you know, questions and wanting to pin blame. Kinda like a tail on a donkey, you ever know that game? Like a party game for children where you cover they eyes and give 'em a tail like a truth and see how close to the donkey's rear end they can stick it when they can't even see the donkey and they been spun round in a circle three times. That's what folks do with truths, so John says. Close they eyes and stick a pin the first place they comes to. Ain't no justice to it. That's what John says.

Jordy

I don't like lightning. Like having a wolf lick all the back your neck when you ain't expecting it.

Art

Please excuse Jordy. Like I said, he's only six. We taught him his letters and how to hold his pen right, but he ain't never been a day in school his whole life. But this all started with him, and John says we have to let him tell it in his own words.

Leeza

EVERYTHING starts with Jordy. Man, that boy ain't nothing but trouble. I was out in Long Field when I hears him hollering, but he hollers a lot. He's small but he's loud, ain't no doubt about that. I don't take much notice sometimes when there's chores to be done. I hears him hollering down by the river and I stop just in case he's fallen in, but no, that's not how it sounds, so I carry on mending the five bar. Then I hears him getting closer, like a storm, still hailing and hollering a whole shower, and he comes running up through Long Field to where I am by the busted gate, and he looks wilder than ever he looked anytime ever before. He tells me I gotta go with him. We gotta find the others and all go, he says. Rhope's dead.

Jordy

Rhope look dreadful. He lying in the mud at the lip of the river, water lapping at him like a tongue.

Thorn

I was working in the loft up in the barn out back, working on bundling the fencing wire. There's a breeze you get up in the loft, that's why I like working up there, no matter what they tell you. That's the reason, it's cooler up in the breeze. Anyway, I was working, I wasn't asleep all, and then Leeza and Jordy come running in, calling for me to come down urgent. So I go down the ladder and they say we have to go find Arthur, but Art could be anywhere. He don't need to tell us all what he be up to, where he at, he being the oldest.

Art

I have responsibilities the others don't understand. The fact of the matter is that after they woke up Thorn from in the loft, they none of them came looking for me at all. Thorn likes to think he's an adult too, him being next oldest by just a year, but as John says, some years are more crucial than others. And that's true. That's why they don't teach high school students in kindergarten or whatever. So they all went down to the river on their own, because that's how Thorn wanted it. He thought he was an adult.

Jordy

Rhope lying in the mud, mud all over, he lying on his back, staring up into the sky with one eye, cos that's how many he had left. Other side of his face look like he been grilled like a beef burger from over at the carnival that time.

Thorn

What Jordy says is about right. Old Mr Rhope was lying on the muddy riverbank where the water spat him up. One eye staring straight up into heaven like he had a clear view, you know, not blocked by the clouds and the firmament and whatnot. The other eye was staring right up close at a dandelion. We found it later. Half his head was frizzed like he been struck by a bolt of lightning right out of the sky.

Leeza

What are the odds of being struck down like that if you don't believe in God? If divine retribution exists, why ain't there more sinners being zapped left, right and centre? How come God is such a lousy shot most of the time? Makes you realise, if you ask me. Ain't said no prayers since.

Art

So old Mr Rhope was dead of natural or divine causes, whichever way your mind turns it, when we found him. Must have been there a while, least since the last storm. That just makes sense. That's science, the way I look at it; no arguing with that. Except there are folks arguing, passing that donkey tale of truth back and forth, waving it in our direction. Want to pin it on us since we just out here alone now Pa's dead. Want to see us gone one way or another so they can take the farm, that's what John says. That's why we gotta write this down. We didn't do nothing but find him.

Jordy

Sky wolf bit him. We didn't kill him.

Thorn

Why would we fry a man till his eye pop out then throw him in the damned river so he washes up on our land? That seems all kind of crazy stupid if you ask me, you know? Turn your damned donkey around, Mr, his tail's on the end of his nose. Damn!

Leeza

Jordy took us down to the stream and showed us the body lying in the mud. Old Mr Rhope, dead as dead. Ugly, not like when they have the coffin propped open in church. His face was burned on one side, eye blown out of its socket like a bulb. I thought he had been there a while because the mud was all dry except round his legs that were still in the water. He looked peaceful, though, in spite of everything. Didn't look like he was damned like the preacher said he would in his final moments. I ain't be listening to the preacher no more anyhow.

Art

I went down to the river later with Thorn when I got back from taking a goat over to the Carver's farm. We went and looked at the body of poor old Mr Rhope, Thorn showing me all the details he had observed previously. Like where that second eye was to be found. Wasn't nothing I could do, nothing I could have done if I'd been there earlier. So that's when I went and told John, and he looked kinda strange when I told him. He said we should write an account of it, and I said I would, and he said, no, it had to be done by all of us in our own way as we remembered it right. Seems to me we all saw the same thing and ain't said nothing different to the next about it all. Some men from the courthouse came and looked and took the body away. Just want to get on with our lives, now, one day at a time. John says to keep the doors locked at night, keep the rifle primed and handy.

Jordy

When there's a storm, the clouds turn from sheep white to wolf black. The sky growls. That old wolf he press his cold nose against your neck and lick all the hairs up straight as hog bristles. That's what must of happened to old Rhope. Wolf found him out, licked him good and got a taste fer him. Scorched him with is hot breath and bit his eye right out his head. Ain't none of us could do that. Preacher calls the sky wolf some other name, but he knows about him alright. Preacher said Rhope had it coming. That all I can tell about it.

Art

Those men from the court house came back about three days after, poking around and asking all kinds of questions about how Mr Rhope came to be where we found him. What did we talk about, had we been arguing, why had he come round. How do you answer questions like that? We didn't invite him to come die in our river.

Leeza

I didn't like the men that came up from town all of a sudden. Nobody used to come around before. Things was peaceful before we found Mr Rhope. These men came sticking their noses into everything. They had really creepy eyes like they were looking through you, like they weren't interested in what you were saying. Like the way a fox looks at grass when he's after the chickens.

Thorn

A couple days later the courthouse men came back. Some went into the house where Arthur was, but some others came snooping round in the barn. I was up in the loft, all quiet, you know, and I watched them. Looking around real interested, opening up sacks and crates, inspecting the machinery, poking about all over. Eventually they came up the ladder to my loft, and I smiled at that. I snuck back all quiet and fetched out the rifle that don't shoot no more, and I sat there, polishing it all methodical, you know, just so they could see I had it and they didn't scare me none. They was real courteous when they came up the ladder and saw the old rifle.

Art

There was all these papers and documents to sign after that, the men talking all business-like and quickfire so I didn't have time to think. I wanted John to see the papers, tell me what I should do, but the men wasn't going to give me time. Then some more men came in from the back, and I looked up and Thorn was following them with the old rifle, carrying it all casual, but also like a warning. And he was grinning. If you don't know Thorn like we do you might not notice. It wasn't an obvious grin, but if you know Thorn, you ain't rarely seen him happier. We all know the gun don't work, but I guess the men weren't aware of that fact. Anyway, it got me the thinking time I wanted as they all up and left of a sudden.

**

Rope

Lois Elsden

She says to me, well why don't you apply to university, and I reply, I'm not clever enough, and if I am I don't want to go.

That's supposed to be the end of it as far as I'm concerned, but it isn't and in the end she has me filling in the forms, endless reams of them and asking things I don't know how to answer. I know what the questions mean, but what shall I answer? What are your favourite subjects, she asks. Swimming and reading, and as far as I know no university does swimming and reading.

I put down swimming and reading anyway, which she translates as teaching English and PE and says why don't I go to teacher training college. I don't want to be a teacher, but she insists. I like Mrs Johnson, she's lovely, and it's nice that she's so interested in me, and wants me to continue my education and have a career, but I do *not* want to be a teacher, it's the last thing I want to do. Being born and brought up in Cambridge makes it an automatic thing to want to go to uni if you're clever enough, but I don't think I am.

I'm feeling doomy as I collect my bike from the cycle sheds and set off up Long Road. I get to the traffic lights and suddenly, instead of heading for home along the backs of the colleges, I turn left and head out of town towards Grantchester. I'll go for a walk by the river. I don't know what to do, I know I don't want to be a teacher, but what else? Being a swimming coach isn't a paid job.

As usual being near (not even on or in the river) the Granta took my mind away from worrying. No point in thinking about what to do when I leave school, ducking beneath the willows, breathing in the sweet, slightly rotten smell of the water, hearing without listening to the sounds of the river, the pops and bubbles, the ducks and moorhens, the flap of a swan's wings, the plop of a water rat dropping into the stream.

I've gone beyond the last cottages of the village, followed the path through the meadow, no cows today, and back onto the path beside the water. I am heading towards Byron's Pool and wish I had my costume with me, wondering if maybe, if there's no-one about, I might strip off and dive in - as naked as Byron himself was when he swam here.

The willows here are virtually in the water, and then I see the rope, the swing rope. I'd forgotten it was here, who knows who tied it, who knows how many people had jumped up, grabbed it, swung out over the river, maybe hands slipping, accidentally on purpose and launching themselves into the river. I feel tempted to do just that, but walk on.

What to do, what to do, I have to do something, I will get a job, but what job, what could I bear to do? Work in Heffers? The hours I have already spent in that book shop, imagine working there and being paid to be there. I stop and watch a family of swans, thinking that maybe working in Heffers would be a possibility. Maybe I should write to the manager.

My thoughts are interrupted by a shout, and I wonder whether to walk on or turn back. I become aware that there are more shouts and not of anyone mucking about, but shouting out more desperately - I think someone is shouting *help help!*

I run back, back towards the willows and there are two girls hugging each other and shrieking and looking at the river. At first all I see are the ripples as if one of the swans has run across the water flapping its wings to take off. But it's not a swan, it's a hand rising, a strand of bright waterweed round its wrist, and a head, mouth open to scream.

I've dived into water a million times, flung myself off the edge of a pool, stretched out across a chlorine surface, but now I throw my arms forwards and launch and fly and swoop and slide into my river.

There's a thrashing struggling body which fights me but I'm stronger and grasp it, despite the skirt of my uniform wind about my legs and my blouse clinging to me. I break the surface and the body is hacking and coughing and I turn on my back, dragging them over, and above me the sky is bisected by the swinging rope.

Proverb

Oliver Patterson's Adventurous Year

Simon Phelps

Oliver Patterson was having an exceptionally good day. The office party had gone very well. A few drinks, a couple of lines of nose candy and, best news of all, a big, fat Christmas bonus. With a broad smile Oliver Patterson jumped out of his taxi and, happily immune to the chilly rain in his quality top coat, strode across the pavement to the ATM.

Meanwhile David Walsh was having an exceptionally bad day. The gas people had dug up the road by his usual begging spot leaving him stranded. He'd been smacked in the face by his dealer after seeking yet another lay on. Shivering, sweating and sniffling miserably he waited for Greasy Colin to leave his spot by the cash machine at the top of Corn Street. Colin worked to the clock, at exactly 6.30 pm he would leave his lucrative rush hour spot and head to the Front Line to score. Finally, he left and David shot into his spot. If he could just beg enough for a rock to get high and then some brown to take him down and stop him clucking. It wasn't hard to look miserable and destitute because that's exactly how it was.

David saw Oliver coming, "Spare a pound for a homeless man, mister?"

Oliver took his wodge of cash from the machine and waved a twenty in front of David's face. David reached out for it, just a fraction too slowly. Oliver snatched it back.

"No, I have a better idea. It's Christmas. You are coming home with me."

David burst into tears as his dream vanished, "I'd rather just have the money mister. Just give me the money."

Oliver dragged him to his feet and pushed him into the taxi. David, who once would have fought for that note was so beaten and weakened, he just gave in. The taxi driver ostentatiously sprayed air freshener around the cab. "If that junkie messes in my cab you'll be charged for it."

Oliver, massively pleased with himself, gave the twenty to the cabby. David descended into sobbing.

They arrived at Oliver's large house in Redland which had recently been converted back from student housing into a luxury family home. Not that the family had come yet but the lower ground floor made Sophie, his wife, an excellent pottery studio with a kiln attached to the back. The two large reception rooms, the large kitchen and the three guest rooms made it a great house for parties and to impress their friends. Oliver and Sophie loved their life.

"Hi Soph, I've brought someone back for dinner."

Sophie walked into the spacious hallway wiping her hands on her apron. "This is rather short notice Olly," she said with a smile in her voice. Then, seeing David, she stopped talking and frowned quizzically at Olly.

"Oh, this is...Yeah, what is your name?"

David, shivering, though not with cold, told them his name.

"I found him by the cash machine sitting in the rain. Christmas, good will to all men, tra la la la eh? I've brought him home for Christmas."

This was news for David. His mind turned furiously. 'I need to get out of here. I need to score.' "Just give me the twenty pounds mister and I'll be gone, please. Just give me some money."

"Hah! Nonsense, you're going to stay with us," said Olly pulling him into the kitchen. David sat on a bar stool beside the polished marble island and wept.

Sophie, who was a compassionate soul, dropped her shock and irritation and ran up to David and put her arms around him. Supressing a shudder as her olfactory senses reeled, she said, "Oh, you poor man. Let's get you into the bath while I prepare some food. Olly pour him a glass of wine while I go and run the bath."

Olly gave him an oversized glass with an undersized amount of wine in it. Looking furtively over his shoulder he lined out some coke on the counter, "Here, snort a line while she's upstairs."

David complied willingly, anything to stave off the chills. He was feeling quite sick now and his guts were churning ominously. Sophie walked back in, "I've run a bath for you. Leave your clothes outside the door and I'll wash them. I've left one of Olly's old dressing gowns in there for you."

She showed him the bathroom. He sank into the warm water gratefully. His legs were beginning to twitch and tense with withdrawals. He reached for the delicately scented soap when a spasm in his gut sent him leaping out of the bath. He reached the toilet just in time for his constipated bowels to open.

After he'd finished and puked up a load of bile from his empty stomach David lay back in the water. All he could think about was heroin. He heard Sophie's voice calling. Getting out of the bath he dried his trembling body then put on the dressing gown and went back to the kitchen.

"My God, you are skinny. You look like a scarecrow in a sheet," declared Olly.

Sophie rushed up to David and sat him down tenderly. Olly felt a small stab of jealousy.

There was food on the table. David picked at it while Sophie ate heartily and Olly, his appetite suppressed by the cocaine, tried hard to look like he was enjoying his plateful.

"I'm sorry," said David, "I can't eat. If I could have my clothes I could be on my way."

"Oh David," said Sophie. "They're so dirty I've put them in the trash. If you can't eat, then why don't you lie down. Perhaps you'll feel better after some sleep."

David knew he wouldn't and there was little chance he'd sleep at all. He knew he was in for a rough night. They went upstairs and Sophie showed him to a bedroom. David climbed into the bed, even through the racking cramps now overtaking his body he delighted in the soft mattress and the clean sheets. Much more comfortable than his dirty corner of the underground carpark and his cardboard box.

He lay there groaning quietly, wide awake. He heard Olly and Sophie go to bed, gave it an hour then got up, slipped on the dressing gown and snuck downstairs. He crept around looking for cash and valuables then realised he had no pockets to put them in. 'Where do they keep the trash?' He found some of Olly's shoes, they fitted perfectly. He put them on his bare feet. His clothes must be in a bin outside. He tried the back door. Suddenly an alarm was blaring and a red-light flashing. 'Oh shit,' he thought, 'I'm in trouble now.'

Sophie and Olly rushed downstairs. Olly took one look at David, turned around, and went back to bed. Sophie and David stayed up all night, talking while David drank cup after cup of very sweet tea.

The next day while Olly was out collecting the organic, free range bronze turkey from the butchers Sophie took David to his first ever Narcotics Anonymous meeting.

Christmas went surprisingly well. David got sicker before he got better but by New Year, he was starting to feel a whole lot more human. Sophie fussed around him like a mother hen. Come New Year's Eve Olly was ready to party.

"Why aren't you ready Sophie? We always go clubbing on New Year's Eve."

"I'm going to stay at home with David. You go, darling," she said as he was dressing, "I don't want David sneaking away."

"Hmmm, I suppose so. Seems a shame though." Once again Olly felt a small twinge of jealousy. He sniffed a bump of snow from what remained in his snappy bag, called a taxi and went out.

Olly had quite a night, hit a couple of clubs under the bottom of Park Street, saw in the New Year on College Green then charged off to the Blue Mountain with a bunch of people he'd never met before. They didn't have much money but they had a lot of drugs. So he paid them in and bought the drinks while they gave him ecstasy and crystal meth. He had a real night to remember. At least in patches.

Two days later he got home feeling miserable and wretched. Sophie was beside herself, absolutely furious, accusing him of taking drugs, which he denied unconvincingly.

"You are not at university now, you know. You need to grow up." Then, walking out of the kitchen where they were arguing, she declared that, "You might as well know David is going to be staying here. He's promised to stay clean, go to meetings and help me in my studio."

As the echoes of the slamming door reverberated Olly drank half a bottle of wine, ate some paracetamol and went up to bed.

Back at work Olly started out well then found himself day dreaming more and more. His mind kept going back to the new year and that funky bunch of people he'd met. Their strange clothes and tattoos and the enchanting woman with the shaved head and the fascinatingly pierced tongue drifted into his mind more and more often as he looked around his office full of besuited men and women with their boring and conventional lives.

Meanwhile Sophie, with David's help was building up a great collection of ceramics, exhibiting in more and more prestigious galleries and was becoming a name in Bristol art circles. She now had objects in galleries in St. Ives, Marlborough, and finally, in March, a show in Kensington. At the opening she insisted on taking David with them. Sophie sparkled in a beautiful dress. David looked great in a linen suit only drinking sparkling water. Olly, despite his expensive suit, looked a little crumpled as he drank a little too much and visited the toilets a little too often for a sneaky line of coke.

On the way back he was bad tempered, rude and belligerent. He came very close to suggesting that Sophie and David were more than just friends. That night, for the first time ever, Olly slept in a spare room.

As the year went on Olly started visiting his dealer more often as well as slipping into The Highbury Vaults for a quick snifter on the way home. His marriage staggered on, neither of them knowing how to deal with the changes in their lives. His work began to suffer. Then one light Friday evening he saw a face he recognised.

"Hey, didn't we meet on New Years Eve on College Green?"

"Yeah, I remember you. You were that funny suit. Ha ha. You liked to party, didn't you?"

"Here, let me get you a pint."

"Thanks, Olly wasn't it?"

"Yeah, your name? I forget."

"Not surprising. You were flying high. Sean, mate."

"Sean, right. You were with that girl. What's her name?"

"I was with a lot of people." Sean laughed, looking sideways with a grin, "Jasmine, at least that's what she calls herself at the moment. Hey, there's a free party on in a warehouse by the docks tonight. Wanna come?"

That was the beginning of a whole new adventure for Olly. Again, he didn't get home the next morning. Again, when he did, he slept in a spare room. On the Monday he felt so wretched he didn't get up for work.

He never got back into his wife's bed. Weekends became what he lived for. Clubs, the cash machine, drugs, the cash machine, raves, the cash machine. Then one day he'd found himself in a squat after party wired with ecstasy and amphetamines, jittery as a bug on a hotplate. Jasmine, who he followed around like a sick puppy, passed him some brown powder on tinfoil and a small glass tube.

"What's that?"

"Just a bit of gear, help you with your comedown. Here let me show you how."

At first Olly couldn't get the hang of it. The smoke kept curling round his ears. Then he got it, and got the hit. Something registered. He felt his whole being calm down. He grinned, "Isn't this stuff addictive?"

"Ah It's alright. Just don't use it too often."

Olly did do it too often. He also started smoking crack and ice. He got more and more paranoid and when he was at home became convinced he could hear David creeping into his wife's room. He'd sit behind his door listening, then hearing a creak, he'd fly out of the door. Only to find no one was there. His work suffered and eventually they let him go. By now he didn't care. The summer was over. He'd been to festivals, parties on traveller's sites, in the woods, on the beach, but he found he'd got less and less interested in the parties. Sean and Jasmine both looked sick and yellow but Olly couldn't see it. As the nights drew in, he felt gloomier. He started scoring alone. Taking his crack and his gear home with him, sneaking into the garage to get high.

David had gone from strength to strength. He'd regularly gone to meetings and got himself a sponsor who was a great support. Sophie had become a great success. Her art work commanded really high prices and was much sought after. Soon she could pay David and cover the mortgage. Things between her and Olly got progressively worse. David had tried to talk to him a thousand times. He knew much better than Sophie what was happening. Then one night Sophie had opened her bedroom door to find Olly knelt listening outside.

"What are you doing here? Olly, what are you doing?"

Olly pushed his way into the bedroom, "He's in here, isn't he? I know he's in here." Olly began crashing around the room, barging into the ensuite bathroom and the walk-in wardrobe. "He must be under the bed."

By now the ruckus had woken David up. He came out of his room to find a distraught Sophie screaming at Olly while he was crawling around the floor absolutely certain he would find David in there somewhere.

Then he saw David, "How did you get past me? How did you get out here?" Then, picking up a lamp and pulling its cable from the wall he attacked David savagely. He hurt David quite badly before David pulled himself together and with his new gym toned strength managed to hold Olly off. Sophie called the police who took Olly away in handcuffs. At David's request, no charges were pressed but after that night Olly never went home again. The whole incident added another layer to Sophie and David's relationship and soon after that, they did, indeed, become lovers.

At first Olly felt like he'd hit the jackpot. He stayed in hotels, saw more and more of his junkie friends who loved him, of course, as he burned through his quite considerable savings. Then suddenly, it was all gone. The hotel kicked him out. He'd wander from crack house to squat, from dealer to dealer to find that people who'd taken thousands of pounds off him would no longer give him the time of day. His heroin habit had grown and grown and, as his money went, he was sick everyday as he could only get just enough to get by. He grew more desperate but he was too scared to steal and too weak to rob. As Christmas approached he took to begging, full of self-loathing as the depth of his humiliation stared him in the face. Then one day he found himself at the top of Corn Street and saw Greasy Colin leave his spot. He quickly ran over to it and sat by the ATM.

A besuited man put his card into the machine.

"Got any spare change mister? Got any spare change for a man who's down on his luck?"

"Not on your nellie, mate. You'll get nothing from me. Don't you know that no good deed goes unpunished?"

Another Turned Page

Lois Elsden

Another fall, another turned page... it wasn't a proverb, but it should have been, if I was American and if I called autumn the fall and the phrase hadn't been written by Wallace Earle Stegner.

I sauntered along, thinking gloomy thoughts, wallowing as young people do, in my misery. I can say that, as I'm no longer young and any gloomy thoughts are different from a twenty-year-old's maudlin ponderings.

It was autumn, a dank, damp, miserable evening and perfect for my feeling of sadness and... and loneliness. A combination of rejection by someone I'd made tentative advances to, and Dr Chivers scrawled note in the margin of my essay - *journalistic bombast!!!* - with the three exclamation marks, had been the latest blows added to my sense of isolation.

The uneven paving stones were wet and shiny, the fallen leaves claggy clumps and all was lit by the nasty yellow glow of the street lamps. I was off the main drag and there was no-one about although it wasn't late. I hadn't really made any friends, although when I wrote home I suggested that I had, and these empty streets just added to my sense of isolation - yes isolation.

I didn't fit, my southern accent was mocked as being posh - actually, not mocked, I was teased. Someone had said 'I'm only joshing!' when my face had obviously given away my feelings, and I didn't know what they meant, and felt foolish. I realised later that I'd embarrassed them as I'd embarrassed myself.

November, the depths of autumn and five whole weeks until the end of term. I plodded on, thinking about the line from the Stegner novel that we'd been ploughing through in American Lit. *Another fall, another turned page...*

Autumn was never a good time for me, I'd had glandular fever when I'd just started at a new school and missed six weeks and never quite caught up with subjects or friends, my dad had left us on Guy Fawkes Night, I'd been dumped one Halloween... I cast around to think of other autumnal miseries which had changed my life, *another turned page.*

I went round a corner and realised I really had no idea where I was. There was a pub just across the road. I had been in a few pubs with people who I was trying to connect with, and had got pissed on the cheap mild, but not this pub, The Strone Pluck, a curious name.

I'm not sure what happened. Maybe it was that the pub door swung open and light and a couple of rowdy people staggered out. Maybe I was just fed up with feeling sorry for myself. Maybe I was thirsty. Maybe a page turned.

I crossed the road and went in quickly before I could think about it too much. Nobody paid me any attention as I pushed through the crowd of rowdy folk. There were people I recognised as students, older people who were obviously locals, the juke box was phenomenally loud, the air was blue with smoke.

There was a crush at the bar and I was squashed at one end, the barmaids at the other. Maybe I would just stand here and not even get a drink, just stand among loud, jolly people, and at least not be on my own.

"Excuse me," someone was actually speaking to me I realised. Standing slightly behind my shoulder so I couldn't really get a look at their face, young, glasses, not a local accent. "Excuse me, can I buy you a drink," a polite, nervous voice.

"No, it's ok," but as I spoke there was a roar of laughter and my voice was drowned.

"... you a drink?"

Just turn the bloody page!

"Yes, yes, thank you, that's very kind, a pint of mild, please."

Somehow drinks were ordered and bought and we struggled away from the crush and found a table beneath a picture of a greyhound race.

"Have you been here before?"

"No, never."

"Me neither," and we exchanged cautious smiles and clinked glasses.

A Stitch in Time Saves Nine

Elizabeth Lawrence

Christmastime twenty-two years ago was cold and grey, sleety and grainy, blurring our vision as we struggled along slippery pavements, the icy wind striking through the gaps of our thick coats. The town's brass band playing carols added some comfort, if a little melancholy, and the multicoloured lights twinkled in the early darkness amidst icy vapours of sea mist and chimney smoke. I felt the old magic blend of Christmas nostalgia and excitement, never quite sharing the cynicism and weariness of some, as my eyes caught ideas for stocking-fillers in the shop windows. My ten-year-old daughter, counting down the days for Santa's arrival down the chimney, had written to him a very short and basic letter. Never a demanding child, I nonetheless wanted to bring her enchantment, but was running out of ideas in our small, Cornish town before the days of online shopping.

Then, entering Tesco with practical matters on my mind, and thankful for the warm air blowing onto my cold face, I encountered a group of huge, white, cuddly toys looking as if they had just arrived from the arctic, perhaps uncharacteristically sent off-course due to the freezing conditions in the south. As I gazed at the group of furry friends, wondering which my daughter would love, it was impossible to choose in such a cuteness overload. Already, my favourite was Pandora, a soft and gentle looking polar bear with a blue satin pouch wrapped around her back containing her little bear cub. Spencer the Seal was also very cute, with his smart and cheerful stance, and a seal pup nestled inside his blue satin backpack. And then Chilly the snowman, sporting a blue satin hat and cape, with a mischievous glint in his eyes. How could I separate the pack seeing as they had already travelled so far together! There was no alternative but to buy one of each and I am quite sure they were smiling as I lifted them one at a time into my trolley. The other shoppers were definitely smiling at the sight of a trolley full of furry friends instead of the food shopping I had set out to do. I was smitten and Christmas Day couldn't come soon enough.

Christmas morning arrived with a fall of perfect, deep snow as we burned logs in the hearth and set the house aglow with fairy lights. Enormous presents are always such fun for a child to unwrap, and my daughter was delighted by their contents as each soft furry friend fell into her lap. With her ensuing 'aahs' we shared in the magic that a child brings to Christmas. She remained snugly buried among them for most of Christmas, watching TV and playing little games in her warm nest. With her pale-pink fleecy dressing gown and white-blonde silky hair it was hard to distinguish her from the soft white toys, as if we had had a litter of pups for Christmas.

Despite being huge, the winter friends lived in her bedroom with all the other toys all year round, and *not just for Christmas*, as the slogan says. With every house move, they always came with us. Eventually, when my daughter was much older, out of sheer practicality we had to store them in the garage in breathable protective bags. We always marvelled at their condition after all these years, keeping their sleek and shiny fur, as fresh-smelling as when they were new. Neither she nor I could ever have given them away, and each Christmas they take up residency again, adorning the living room, draped over the furniture and nestled into on cold evenings. They seem to come to life as they read over our shoulders and listen to our chatter.

This year, in a splurge of clearing the garage, the winter friends were allowed back in the house for a while. On close inspection, we were dismayed to see that Pandora's fur had burst open and soft white stuffing was escaping from her chest. And even worse – she appeared to have mouse droppings in her fur! We were horrified and could only imagine her terror at being eaten alive by a little rodent, hell-bent on securing an ultra-soft nest and eventually having to eat its way out. It seemed her eyes had become wild and unfocused, and even Spencer and Chilly looked upset as they all grouped protectively together. I did my best to patch her up, replacing the stuffing and stitching her wound. I promised to give them all a pampering beauty session with a sponge-clean, brush and airing soon.

The following week, as I came down to breakfast one morning, I was met by the sound of my daughter shrieking. Pandora had been attacked again and there were several tears across her whole body. We could hear scratching and scrabbling coming from the baking cupboard. Opening the cupboard door a couple of inches ajar, bracing ourselves for what we knew would be there, we were met by the sight of burst sugar and flour bags, and nine tiny baby mice scuttling around. We concluded that they must have been born within Pandora and I had stitched them inside her body! We released the young into a hedge in a nearby park, assuming they could now fend for themselves. Shortly after, we caught the mother mouse in a humane trap and took her to the same hedge, imagining a happy rodent reunion.

    I don't blame the mice for trying to find refuge from the cold temperatures outside. I remember the last freeze, when we first moved to these supposed warmer climes. Night time temperatures dropped to minus fifteen degrees, causing all the water pipes to freeze. A wader bird nested in the drain under the kitchen window, making such a racket sorting out its nest each evening, treading straw round and round in circles. Animals have to somehow survive the harsh winters.

    As Spencer looked after Pandora's cub, I performed emergency surgery, carefully stitching all her wounds. Chilly stayed by her bedside and cheered her up until she had recovered. After a thorough clean and airing in the spring sunshine, she was as good as new and reunited with her baby. We faithfully promised our winter friends that never again would they have to live in the garage at the mercy of mice. After all their years of bringing us joy, they had earned a peaceful retirement in the spare bedroom, coming back to warm our hearts again every Christmas.

The Customer is Always Right

Macaque

"I've got a proverb for you, a nice modern one. Businessman goes to one of those Prêt-à-Manger or Soho Coffee cabins, you know the ones they have in airports and railway stations – they do everything the main outlets do, but they just have one or two people working there, you know? So, the guy goes up to the counter and sits on one of the stools, just as an older woman who has been talking to a young man at the back of the kiosk leaves through a side door. The young lad, maybe 18, fresh faced, crisp polo shirt, asks what the customer would like, and the customer says he would like a cheese sandwich.
- We're not doing cheese sandwiches today, I'm afraid, Sir.
- I'm sorry? Says the customer, looking up at the signage to make sure he hasn't accidentally approached the Dunkin' Donut concession.
- There's no need to apologise, Sir, says the boy, with great sincerity.
- No, I mean 'what do you mean you're not doing cheese sandwiches?'
- We're not selling them today, Sir, we don't have any left. Can I get you something else? He's very polite and professional, upright bearing, kind smile, smart new apron.
- Right, says the customer, looking at the laminated menu on the counter. Are you still doing the toasted cheese?
- Yes, Sir, would you like that instead?
- So, you've got bread...enquires the customer.
- Yes.
- And you've got cheese...
- Yes, replies the boy, seemingly unaware of where this line of inquiry might be leading.
- So, you can toast some bread, slice some cheese, and put the cheese on the toast and melt it...
- Yes, Sir.
- But you're not selling cheese sandwiches at the moment.
- That's right, says the boy, determining that, in spite of the sharp suit and the briefcase, this man must be a little slow on the uptake.
- Okay, I'll take two of the cheese on toast, please. Lightly toasted, not too dark.

- Certainly, Sir, replies the infant, aware that people with learning difficulties often have to have things done a certain way or else suffer a breakdown.
He dutifully prepares the toast, watching the colour closely, and heats the cheese just enough to soften it and not liver-spot it, which is how he likes it himself.
- There we are, Sir, two cheese on toast, and he places two small plates before the businessman, who, in his turn, takes one of the slices of toasted cheese and inverts it over the other one, pressing it firmly down with satisfaction, saying 'Hey, presto! A cheese sandwich!'
- That will be £7.90 please, Sir, says the boy.
- What for? asks the man.
- That, erm, cheese sandwich.
- But you're not selling cheese sandwiches today, says the man, and with his lunch in one hand and his briefcase in the other, he departs, leaving the poor, incredulous boy looking stupefied."

"Well, that sounds more like a parable or a fable to me; what's the proverb to extrapolate from that tale? The customer is always a smart-arse?"

"I suppose it's 'If you've got bread and cheese, make a sandwich.'"

"A bit obscure, but it works, I suppose. So, what happens when the manager returns and the trainee has to explain what happened?"

"She took £5.00 out of my wages. Staff discount."

Need to Know

Brian Price

The inquiry cleared me, personally, and I didn't even have to use the Nuremburg defence – that I was only following orders. Emails and records of meetings and conversations, which I had prudently retained, got me off the hook, at least legally, and laid the blame clearly at the doors of company management and certain corrupt officials in other countries. But still…

It wasn't my idea in the first place. It was the kind of thing people speculated about in the bar at conferences. How to develop a new food which could grow anywhere and provide an almost complete meal. New Scientist magazine occasionally ran speculative articles on the topic, as well as featuring similar ideas in a cartoon strip, which ran in the magazine during the 1970s. But the Director of our lab must have picked the idea up, thought about it over a few drinks, and pitched it to several biotechnology companies. Against all odds, one of them picked it up.

I tried to explain about the knowledge gap. We knew a lot about manipulating genes. After all, we'd been doing it since the last century. But this was different. The idea was to insert drought-resistance genes, from a new, engineered, strain of wheat, into a potato, as well as lentil genes, which would increase the protein content. Adding a few tomato genes could boost the vitamin C levels and maybe a few bean genes would produce folic acid. Some clover could enable it to produce its own fertiliser, by attracting bacteria to the crop's roots which would fix nitrogen from the air. The result would be a highly nutritious potato crop, that could grow in a wide variety of environments. Coincidentally, it would also be ideal for making crisps, or chips as our backers called them. They had already been trademarked as "Magachips". Less frivolously, the crop could provide extremely valuable nutrition for people in a wide range of countries.

What we didn't know was how to combine such a range of genes in the same organism, without causing problems. Would they be compatible? Would one lot cancel out the other? Were we simply getting above ourselves with a pick'n'mix approach to genetics? Knowledgeable as we were about the subject, there were massive areas of ignorance. But we were well-funded, by people who believed that throwing money at a problem would automatically solve it. Clearly, they weren't scientists.

So, we attacked the problem, day and night, working in shifts. As I suspected, trying to shove all these alien genes into the humble potato didn't work. Either the plant didn't grow at all, or it produced weird vegetables which proved inedible. Genetically speaking, it looked like too many cooks were spoiling the spud. The problems kept all the senior scientists on the project awake at nights, as well as a good few of the junior ones. We tried using promoter genes – those which made other genes do their job – from all the plants involved but that made no difference. Then I had an idea. Every organism has loads of junk DNA – stuff which doesn't seem to do anything. Perhaps the answer was there?

I spent weeks mucking around with DNA from all the plants involved, culturing cells in the lab rather than growing the full crops, in order to save time. I did occasionally ask myself whether it was worth it. Perhaps we didn't need to know how to do such bizarre things as this. Eventually, I found something promising and produced the first Superspud. Somehow, I knew it would work. Hubris, indeed.

So, we grew a test crop in a secret, closely guarded field in Lincolnshire, and ran the usual animal tests. I'd never seen such healthy, well-nourished lab rats as those fed on our creation. We did chemical tests to make sure the desired nutrients were present, and also ruled out many undesirable substances. Green lights, throughout. But there was still a major trial to be done. Could humans eat Superspuds?

I tried to explain to our backers that there could be problems. That we shouldn't rush things. This was a completely new food, after all. But the American company was desperate to get the product to market ahead of their Chinese rivals who, it was rumoured, were working along the same lines.

"Don't worry," they said. "We don't have to do the tests in Europe or the US. There's plenty of countries in Africa or Central America where we have influence. They'll welcome a couple of schools and the odd hospital, in return for letting us run a few speedy field trials."

So, we grew several tonnes of Superspuds, producing seed potatoes for trials in a small Central American country. Initial results showed that they grew quicker than expected, and publicity videos circulated by the company showed bountiful yields. Hundreds of people eagerly came forward to try them. All was looking well, and the lab Director was rumoured to be preparing her Nobel Prize acceptance speech.

The next videos didn't come from the company, though. They came from activists and, eventually, from mainstream news media. And they paralysed me with horror.

You see, the potato is closely related to the Deadly Nightshade plant. This was of little significance in the chilly fields of Lincolnshire but, in the warmer soils of Central America, a particular gene unexpectedly switched on. The gene that produces the deadly poison, atropine. I will never forget those images of children and adults, stumbling around outside the test canteens, barely able to see, gasping for water, hallucinating and tearing their clothes off as they overheated.

The project was abandoned, the company was prosecuted and our lab was closed down, fortunately without anyone going to prison. But someone, obviously a disgruntled employee, had graffitied a few words on the boarded-up building, words which I could only agree with. Knowledge may be power, but when ignorance is bliss, 'tis folly to be wise.

Recording

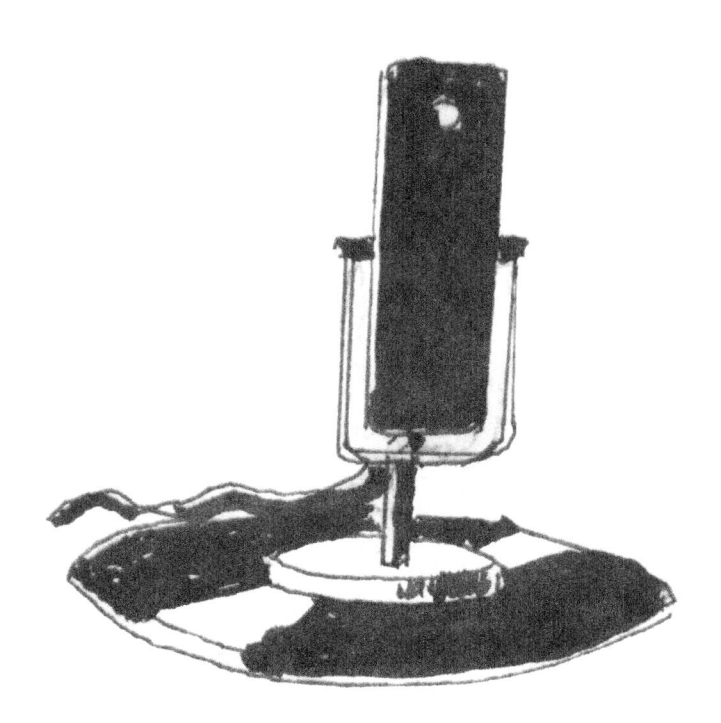

For the Record

Macaque

"Going once; going twice; are we all done in the room?" The gavel smacked down smartly and the lot was hers. Niki released the breath she had been holding, and unclenched her tingling fists. She felt dizzy with the sudden release of tension, and took a few moments to recover before settling up and collecting her purchase.

In a hospital in Leningrad in 1965, Viktor had been a porter. Young, dark, fit and intelligent, he had been popular, putting patients of all walks of life at ease. He was polite and respectful, kindly and entertaining with the children, a little flirtatious, perhaps, with the women, conspiratorial with the men, and always happy to help the doctors, nurses and admin staff with whatever he could. His hair and clothes were modern, and he sometimes offered friends Western brands of cigarettes, but he was young, studying at the university, the spirit of the sixties was beginning to be felt even here in Mother Russia. He never gave any outward indication of being a radical or subversive; he lived with his mother, did her shopping, could be seen walking with her on his arm in their neighbourhood. Viktor was as close to being above suspicion as anyone in the USSR. And he never objected to emptying the bins.

"Viktor," called Dr Aronofski, "these must be incinerated immediately. Understand?"

"Da. Understood, Doctor."

"Good. I have an important engagement. How is your mother?"

"She will outlive us all, sir."

"Good. Good." Shrugging on his overcoat and pulling up the collar, the doctor swept into the corridor. "Goodnight, Viktor," he called, as the doors swung to behind him. Viktor glanced at the name on the manilla folder, then looked nervously about him. He quickly slipped two of the x-rays into the lining of his lab coat, then added the folder to the sacks of rubbish on his trolley, and headed to the furnace room.

A week later, with the x-rays now concealed in the lining of his overcoat, he sat in the back corner of the Korova bar listening to the awful Russian music, a textbook open in front of him, waiting for his contact. He always felt nervous in these situations, and was already on his fourth vodka when Dmitri joined him with a loud pretence of not having arranged the meeting.

"Viktor! I wondered if I might bump into you somewhere!" He removed his hat, coat and scarf, and sat down, gesturing to the barman for some vodka. "I wanted to ask you about that girl you were with the other night," he said, as the barman came over to the table. Looking out from his corner, Viktor could see that nobody was taking an interest in either of them, nor the fact that they were meeting. As they continued to talk in lowered voices, Viktor relaxed and only sipped at his last glass. Then the two of them stood up, surreptitiously donning each other's overcoats, and walked out of the bar and up the street together before parting, Viktor on foot back to his apartment, Dmitri on the tram heading towards the university.

"Is that you, Vitya?" his mother called as he closed the door to the apartment, easing the handle gently into the catch in an attempt to be clandestine.

"Da, Mamochka. Is anything the matter?"

"It's late. I was worried. Did you fetch the bread?"

He went into her room and kissed her forehead, showing her the loaf and some cheese he had procured. "I'll fill the samovar, make us some tea."

While the ancient samovar was heating the tea, Viktor went into his own room and opened the secret pocket in the lining of the coat. He reverently withdrew the sheet of mottled acetate. He was curious about the process, but the less he knew about what and who was involved the better. All he did know was that he was a small yet vital cog in the machine that was helping to modernise his country; he was working for the good of the people, and now so was Krushchev. The president had been progressive in fits and starts since coming to power, but the KGB still had their hands around Mother Russia's throat.

Viktor held the x-ray by the edges and turned it to the weak crepuscular light nudging through the window. Etched on the image of a rib cage was an almost imperceptible groove spiralling out from a hole in the centre. He very carefully placed the hole over the spindle on his turntable and lifted the arm, lowering the needle onto the outer edge of the spinning groove. These moments were precious to Viktor. This would be his one chance to hear what the rest of the world could enjoy any time they liked. Each of these recordings, bone music as they were known on the streets, would wear out after half a dozen plays, so Viktor could only listen to the song once before selling it to a client on the black market. He felt entitled to this one liberty, being the source of most of the x-rays that his contacts at the university used.

The needle crackled, and Viktor felt an electric charge of anticipation in the microcosm of his small room, then notes from a guitar emerged, an almost unmetered, syncopated rhythm, free and unstable and mesmerising. The crackle from the needle was constant, but the music was clear enough; voices sang in English, beyond Viktor's comprehension at that speed, but it was that writhing, snaking guitar riff that held his attention, and when it moved up a fifth in the blues progression, he thought his heart would stop. There followed a chorus of chords that croaked angrily through the static of the needle, and then the riff was taken up again by a single guitar, and now cymbals, and the second verse. Viktor realised that each of the lines sung was repeated, and given more time he would have been able to understand more of the lyrics, but here he was, at the forefront of modern Russia, listening to brand new music by the Beatles, revolutionary music, and it was thanks in part to him that just a few people in similar small rooms around the city would get to hear it too. Thanks to him, and to Nikita Krushchev, for the ribs and lungs on this x-ray belonged to the president.

It was as he was preparing to take the latest batch of bone records to his client that Viktor noticed that the same mark that appeared on Kruschev's left lung also appeared on two other images, one of a fractured ulna, and another of a patella. The x-rays had been taken within a day of each other, but the patients were all under different doctors, and in the cases of the broken bones, it had been on the margin of the image. He plucked up the courage to mention to Dr Aronofsky that whilst incinerating the acetates in question he had noticed the anomaly that wouldn't have been spotted by the individual doctors, and consequently received the gratitude of the president in his relief at being given an unexpected clean bill of health. He and his mother were able to move to a better apartment and enjoy more luxuries, and he continued to help create and circulate bone music around the city. After his mother's death he moved to England, but not before the Beatles had disbanded. He worked as a hospital porter until he had saved enough to open a music shop, and amassed a spectacular record collection of his own.

Viktor was sitting in his study, listening to Cream playing live at the Albert Hall in 1968, when Niki came to see him. An old samovar sat on his desk next to a black and white photo of a couple on their wedding day, and all the walls were lined from floor to ceiling with vinyl records in sixteen-by-eight-inch apertures in the wooden shelving he had made himself. None of the shelves were labelled, but Viktor knew where every single record was by heart.

He stood up to greet her with a big smile. "Come through, Nikita," he said, "I'll make some tea with jam."

"I'll have coffee, Dad," she said.

"Fsht!" exclaimed the old man, "just like your mother."

Niki contained her excitement while her father made the coffee and his traditional Russian tea, and then, when they were seated at the kitchen table, she produced the slim cardboard box that she had spent years searching for.

"I think this might be," she said, leaving the sentence unfinished, nerves and expectation making her hands shake as she passed it to him.

Viktor opened the box and parted the folds of tissue paper, then stared at the sheet of acetate before him.

"Da, Nikita," he said slowly, pushing the box aside to protect it from his tears.

Water, My Blood

Elizabeth Lawrence

    Spring had arrived, and very welcome too after a typical British winter of grey skies, chilly winds and enough precipitation to hopefully fill the reservoirs for the whole year ahead. I embraced the softer air, noticing a little warmth in the weak sunlight as I breathed in the earthy scents of wild garlic and fresh grass, exhaling gentle sighs of relief; my recent headaches and tiredness surely now banished with the winter. The dappled sunlight shone through the bare branches of tall trees. Even the squirrels were scampering in a playful way once again. Alarmed by a sudden nosebleed, I quickened my pace for home, tissue in place.

    The next evening, walking to singing practice with my friend, we shared our news from the week as usual. She was sounding relieved about her high blood pressure having been diagnosed and treated. She had been experiencing tiredness, headaches and nosebleeds. This made alarm bells ring in my head, knowing I had been negligent about monitoring my own blood pressure after raised readings a year ago. My friend assured me that there is a marvellous walk-in service at Boots pharmacy for this very thing! Well, the thought of any medical intervention was daunting to me, but this sounded low-key and friendly enough for me to give it a try.

    The next day, as part of a reconnoitre around town, I drifted into a quiet Boots and asked if I could have my blood pressure taken. A very serious pharmacist led me into a small room and asked for many details which he studiously entered on a form. I was still feeling fairly relaxed and thinking more about a pot of tea in my favourite coffee shop afterwards. After taking 3 readings with a few minutes' interval between each, he calmly told me that I needed a GP appointment straight way, which he would try to arrange, and if that was not possible, he advised that I should go to A & E without delay. I was allowed to go to my favourite café and wait but not to drink any strong coffee.

    Thinking there must be some mistake and still not too worried, I popped into Coffee#1, my home from home. As I was lining up the pots to pour my tea, my phone suddenly rang. The background music in the café was so loud, I could not hear the voice on the line. One of my dear baristas turned down the volume when I asked, looking surprised at my tense expression. Leaving my hot tea, collecting my bags and throwing on my coat, I arrived at the doctors' surgery just 15 minutes later.

My blood pressure was still crazily high and I was given strict instructions to take readings and record them 4 times daily for a fortnight and to call if the readings surpassed a certain limit. Naively, I said with a smile that they surely would not, to which the doctor retorted that they might. Despondently, I queued for my meds, filled with dread about taking them. I tend to react to most chemicals severely, once almost fatally and I have had difficulty swallowing tablets ever since. But I was starting to realise just how serious severely high blood pressure is and the need to lower it. I had no choice but to take the meds. To my relief, I could swallow them easily, mostly because they quickly dispersed in the mouth.

For the next two weeks, I meticulously recorded all my readings, astonished by the wide variation. It became a source of fascination. My chart was something that any maths teacher would have been impressed by, with its neatly ruled lines and highlighter pens denoting the different levels, whilst also recording any symptoms such as headaches etc. I was super-organised.

Becoming acutely aware of how stress affected the readings, even slight tension or worry, I started to examine my life and everyone in it. I became hypersensitive in all situations, questioning and tearful. In short, I was afraid. Blood is, after all, our lifeline! I felt hypertensive, acutely aware of any pressure building, despite its sinister reputation as a 'silent killer'. The headaches and fatigue continued worse than ever and my mood was, uncharacteristically, very low. A kind friend, mopping up my tears one day, reassured me that the meds can play havoc with mood and hormones, having witnessed her husband's despair when first diagnosed. Usually quick to see the humour in most situations, I had become insular and anxious. I was barely present at times in my social groups; everyone seemed so carefree and light-hearted, and I truly imagined that I wouldn't be with them for much longer. It was as if I had already died and were a visiting ghost, observing how life would go on without me. I felt very sad, but happy for them, such lovely people. My 'sense of self' had disappeared; I was so locked in with dread and symptoms. We take good health for granted and usually enjoy moments without the feelings of dread and morbidity I was experiencing. All kindness and empathy were met by my tears of relief that someone understood and cared enough about me to offer reassurance.

I somehow got through the next fortnight, with the sound of the blood pressure machine buzzing away becoming as familiar as the clock ticking at home, and even the dog took no notice after her initial curiosity. The 2 weeks of meds were nearly over. When I tried to arrange a GP appointment, I was told by the receptionist that I had been referred to a pharmacist instead and would only have a telephone appointment. I was devastated, needing so much reassurance. I wanted to speak to my GP and felt so fobbed off with the pharmacist and receptionist; my husband commented that it would be the window cleaner next! Nonetheless, the pharmacist was very positive about my readings and dismissed the headaches and low mood as an adjustment to the meds. I was relieved and felt that, finally, I could relax.

There was light at the end of the tunnel - an Ostara break for Mother's Day at Centre Parcs, just an hour's drive away. I had been seriously wondering if I would be up to an adventure holiday with my energetic and zestful daughter. But after getting the all clear from the pharmacist, I was able to enjoy a lovely and much needed break, just the tonic I needed, both fun and relaxing. Of course, the blood pressure machine, meds and charts went with me, and my daughter was so thoughtful, carrying heavy bags and making sure I didn't tire.

A couple of days after our return, I was alone at home washing up after lunch when the room seemed to be spinning, my heart thumping and my head very hot. It was frightening not knowing what was happening. I instinctively went outside and sat in the garden with my head between my knees. But the world was still spinning. I was relieved when my daughter came home. Ever a hypochondriac, she was already Googling symptoms and contemplating my end-of-life care! Her worst fears seemed to have manifested before her eyes and I was trying to keep us both calm while thinking what to do. I took my blood pressure, which had surpassed the high-risk level recording, so I rang the surgery. Being caller number 5 in the queue, it was a long wait. Finally, the receptionist informed me there were no appointments that day. When I pleaded that I didn't want to have a stroke while waiting for one, she suggested ringing 111. I did so immediately and from then, the NHS became the organisation we are proud of.

The phone was ringing back within minutes, but in our panic and general ineptitude for technology, neither my husband nor I were capable of pressing the right buttons and we managed to reject 2 calls! When at last I successfully answered the phone to a doctor from the emergency team, she asked lots of questions about my symptoms and then advised me to get to A & E immediately. Rather than risk waiting 7 hours for an ambulance, my very anxious husband would drive me there. As I got ready upstairs, I knew we were in for a long day and goodness knows what they would find. I packed my book to read. I could hear the reassuringly familiar sounds of my husband and daughter bickering about whether or not he should eat his lunch before we left. She stayed working from home, sorting the laundry, making our bed and keeping the dog company.

They were expecting me at the hospital. I had my own room near the ward desk and was monitored for 8 hours with ECGs, blood tests, blood pressure readings and a CT scan. Everyone was very kind and attentive. The triage nurse - a down to earth scouser and dead ringer for Gerry Marsden ('Pacemakers' irony noted!) - told me to just enjoy the ride, have a bit of 'me time', watch the real-life production of Casualty being laid on around me, and that they would sort me out so I mustn't worry. Alice, the duty house doctor, young and enthusiastic with crinkly black hair that had a life of its own, certainly inspired confidence. Her piercingly blue eyes shone with intelligence. The young nurse looking after me complained of his own hot flushes and admired my UGG boots wondering how comfy they were and if he should get some. He noted all my crystal jewellery and shared his wisdom about the different stones such as rose quartz; we were best friends in no time. The staff nurse reminded me so much of my mother, calm and quiet of manner, very thoughtful and serious. She expertly took blood with barely a scratch and ministered aspirin as a precaution. Her hands were so gentle they made me feel precious, and I thought about the healing power of touch. Like many, she was the epitome of womanhood, an angel in blue. I was transported everywhere, most skilfully and attentively, by stretcher, and was starting to feel in full patient mode, remembering my own nursing experience on the wards many years ago, the intimacy of care, which was a privilege to carry out and ultimately very rewarding.

I was so relaxed on the comfy bed and just wanted to read and sleep. My husband wouldn't leave my side, so frightened by the high blood pressure readings, which I didn't want to know. He was making me feel very tense, sitting rigid in his seat watching everything in the corridor, unable to concentrate on any conversation. In the end, I persuaded him to go home, have dinner and walk our dog, assuring him I would be ok for an hour or so.

The evening shift, usually quieter and even cosy on the main wards, was very entertaining in A&E, with the arrival of a classic drunk shouting at everyone and locking himself in the loo. I had been wanting to spend a penny for a while, but it would have involved detaching my ECG wires and I hadn't wanted to bother the busy nurses. Finally, I realised I needed to go quite soon within the realms of decency. I was told that the intoxicated man was still occupying the nearest loo but there was another toilet at the far end of the corridor. I set off unsteadily, only to find two elderly ladies chatting away in the queue. Realising I would be waiting a while, I turned back to take my chances with the drunk. By then, he had been removed and the area fully cleaned with disinfectant, a fervent Romanian nursing assistant assured me. Another angel, this time in a dark ponytail, he told me of his hardships and this being his only chance to better himself in life. His studies for a nursing course and the long shifts take their toll and he feels permanently tired. But so efficient and hardworking; he will be an asset to the profession.

The CT scan and the blood tests were normal, thankfully, and my blood pressure eventually dropped. Doctor Alice discharged me with instructions to take aspirin for two weeks and not to drive. Exercise would be ok though, she told me enthusiastically, and I could even go running and cold-water swimming! I could well imagine her engaging in such pursuits, her eyes still twinkling after a long day. My reality, as I lay sprawled on the bed, was sheer exhaustion. A referral to the mini-stroke clinic was made and I was free to leave. We got home at 10:30pm, where my daughter had been waiting up with a snoring dog, and had a very late dinner.

Duly, the following day, with my husband by my side, I attended my appointment at the mini-stroke clinic. The consultant asked many searching questions, studied all my well documented recordings and was amazed by their variations. He was of the opinion that the meds were probably not agreeing with me. He gave me the all clear to drive. He didn't think I had had a stroke and advised that I stop taking aspirin. This was a massive relief as the damned tablets were burning my whole digestive tract! I was glad to tell my daughter, who was deciding which songs to play at my funeral, that all was well.

So what next? Would I now be seen by my GP as an urgent case to change meds? Would they now see the discrepancy between a phone chat with a pharmacist and a face-to-face appointment with a GP, who might have come to the same conclusion as the consultant weeks ago, avoiding all the subsequent drama and frayed nerves? No one seemed to be in any rush to rectify my problems. If I were the Princess of Wales, I grumbled, I would have been thoroughly reviewed and sorted by a team of top specialists within the hour. My heart sank to think that I would just have to keep taking the wrong meds while I waited for an appointment.

Nearly a week later, I saw my GP who seemed completely unaware of my recent ordeal. She was happy with my recordings overall and, despite the blips, felt I was no longer at risk. I was dismayed when she advised that I stay on the meds - I reiterated about my low mood, headaches and fatigue, but she didn't seem to consider them side effects. She looked amazed at my readings and, apart from the 2 blips, thought they fell within safe limits. We discussed how to raise my mood with a few changes to my life, including counselling, something I had not considered before taking the meds. But even then, no referral was made.

Afterwards, as I queued at the pharmacy for a repeat prescription, my GP reappeared by my side. "May I borrow you?" she asked. I followed her back into her room and she shut the door. "It's possible you might have a rare condition!", her eyes shone with interest.

"I wouldn't be surprised", I answered feebly.
"It's called 'volatile blood'".
"Very likely, with my Welsh and Irish roots".
"The test is a little complicated…"
"Oh yes?"
"You have to collect urine for 24 hours. But we provide the container," she seemed delighted to report.

I had to think about this for a few seconds. "So, I won't be able to take my dog for long walks, reliant as I am on bushes! And I won't be able to pop to town. And then, seriously, will I have the embarrassment of sloshing a heavy container into reception?" This was becoming farcical now.

"Yes, that's about it", she grinned. We could at least share a joke.

"Thanks for that" I replied with sarcasm, and left her excited at the prospect of successfully diagnosing a rare condition.

And so I resignedly picked up the pieces of my life but with trepidation. It took a few days for me to emerge. I was still licking my wounds and recovering from the ordeal, feeling very inward, protecting my very core. I felt a seismic change happening. I was reminded of having just given birth, or recovering from anaphylaxis;

moments of being close to death but surviving, events big enough to break down normality and strip life back to the very basics. The brain remembers past traumas, and reacts similarly to new perceived threats. I felt a strong need to be with my nearest and dearest and they with me. I wanted to see close friends and family and talk through events and my newfound feelings and reviewed outlook on life. The few friends I met saw me as very tired, pale and drawn. I realised who my people were, those who loved and cared about me, who would be devastated to lose me, the ones who were always there for me through thick and thin. The shock reactions as people found out about my brush with the other side was very heartwarming; I experienced such love and support.

Another little episode of raised blood pressure and giddiness occurred, less than before but enough to contact the GP. This time, she suggested I come off the tablets as they were obviously not suiting me, and stopping all the regular recordings. Perhaps she had finally read the consultant's report! I was advised to take random readings of 10 over a week and check in with her then. My readings stayed fairly low and mostly within a normal range. Lifestyle changes seemed to bring down the blood pressure - eliminating stress, prioritising relaxation, and a good balance between rest and exercise.

I became aware that my body was highly reactive to emotions and easily became stressed. I knew I needed to make relaxation and fitness a priority. I learnt how to better manage my life and my stress-detecting antennae were on high alert. But more than that, life really slowed down and became more precious. Mere mortals, we rely on our bodies. I feared it might have been my time to depart, or worse, live a paralysed life. The shock took a long time to wear off.

The harshness of early spring mellowed into late spring. My daughter and I went to Glastonbury for the ancient festival of Beltane, and I was touched by the pagan spirit and reconnection with nature. Women of all ages were fully embracing the day, some even older than me performing to the crowds. I watched them singing, dancing, banging drums, and felt such inspiration and reaffirmation of life. As the revellers chanted "Air my breath, and fire my spirit, earth my body, water my blood," the power and rawness of it all deeply resonated with me.

My joie de vivre returned and I so wanted to live! I longed for the cliffs and waves crashing beneath, sweet gorse and birdsong, and I would sing to myself, *'Low lie the fields of Athenry, where once we watched the small free birds fly. Our love was on the wing, we had dreams and songs to sing. It's so lonely round the fields of....*' I wanted my carefree freedom back and the confidence of youth. Perhaps now, after such a wakeup call, I will live to a ripe old age and the angels will take me one night in a deep and peaceful sleep.

One year later and after a few more blips and episodes, I am back on blood pressure medication and also anti-anxiety pills, which I am hoping to phase out soon. The former cause fatigue and giddiness, which no longer bother me. A minor heart defect has been discovered which explains my erratic blood pressure, and can be managed without restricting activity. I still listen to *The Fields of Athenry* as it plays every morning in the house (and we can't work out how to make Alexa stop this routine!). I have more memories to make and memoirs to write. A record of my life, not my blood pressure. I avoid all readings and recordings now; with a new que sera sera attitude to life and a deeper appreciation, I feel my old optimism retuning, with a newly acquired carapace of resilience. We are more than just recordings, facts and figures. We react according to our individuality and the vicissitudes of life, ever changing, flowing and dynamic, like water. *Water, my blood.*

Stone Tapes

Lois Elsden

"Is it switched on," Sketchley asked over his shoulder. Of course it bloody was, I hadn't lugged all this stuff up here just to not switch it on 'in situ' as Sketchley expressed it. I didn't say that, I just said yeah it was switched on. These were the days when equipment was big, and heavy, very heavy.

Jess was standing slightly behind one of the big lamps which she'd carried up but her face was in shadow. I sensed she was smiling in her enigmatic way. She was pleasant and friendly, but I hadn't got a proper sense of her somehow. Did she think this was all a load of old nonsense too? Or did she think Sketchley was on to something? Obviously, he wasn't, despite all the equipment which had cost him god knows how much. Unlike the rest of us, Sketchley had very wealthy parents.

Hampson, standing beside Sketchley, and holding onto some instrument or other glanced at me; her name was Enid, but everyone called her Hampson. Her look suggested we'd have more than a few pints when we got back tomorrow.

Steve nudged me. "Bloody freezing, mate," he whispered.

"Silence!" ordered Sketchley, and I could have burst out laughing but concentrated on looking at the ichosimeter.

I had the other big lamp behind me so I could read the ichosimeter and record any unusual activity. It would measure any sound in whatever it was attached to, in this case, the castle walls. The meter was supposed to be attached to the sound pads on the wall but Sketchley wanted me to hold it and have my eye on it.

So, here we were, on a very cold November night, in the lower chambers of the hilltop ruins of Gorman's Gaston, a centuries old castle with a reputation for being haunted. We weren't looking for ghosts, however, we were conducting Sketchley's scientific and electronic investigation to try and find audible evidence of those who had once lived here.

You may wonder how it all started. It was innocent enough, in actual fact; we were all members of the Uni film club and became friends in the bar after watching the weekly film. A subset of us got together on a different evening as well, meeting in Sketchley's flat. We would bring our own booze and watch other stuff, vintage and niche stuff which included an old 1970's TV series called 'The Stone Tape'.

It was no longer very frightening, but it had its moments. It was the story of a group of scientists investigating the stone tape theory which is an actual thing. The stone tape theory is the idea that ghostly apparitions and apparent hauntings are in fact analogous to other modern sound recordings. According to Sketchley, they are like a recording of stressful mental experiences, such as might happen during emotional or traumatic events. All this mental energy can actually be projected somehow through some sort of brain power and in effect be recorded in any surrounding stone. Like stone walls in a castle, which was why we were in Gorman's Gaston, trying to replay and hopefully re-record events which had happened here centuries past.

Yeah, crazy.

Sasha was crouched down fiddling with some other piece of equipment. I couldn't tell you what it was. I'm totally ignorant of anything technical and with zero interest, I was only here because these were my only mates - I hadn't really made any other friends, even though I'd joined the footie team, the debating society and the film club. And I quite fancied Sasha.

There were eight of us, just as well with all the bloody equipment. Tank, who was the nearest thing to a mate that Sketchley had, lumbered in with a great big something followed by Smith and Pierre. They didn't appear to be carrying anything.

Tank put the thing down and began to say it was absolutely Baltic but was immediately shushed by Sketchley. Down in this bit of the ruin, in what seemed to be a cellar, and out of the roar of the wind and all the various creaky stormy noises of a wild night, it actually was very quiet, creepy quiet. I had an urge to giggle and stared hard at my ichosimeter.

"Will you cut it out!" Sasha said unexpectedly and angrily, and I think we all jumped.

"What's the matter, Sash?" Jess asked, as Sketchley was demanding silence.

"Whoever it is who keeps pushing me."

"There's no-one near you, we're all over here," said Steve. He fancied Sash too, I could tell.

Several people were speaking at once, and Sasha stood up and stomped over to Steve, a strange look on her face.

"I guess I just spooked myself," she said, grumpily, but actually I think she'd got the creeps.

"I can hear something!" Sketchley squeaked, and spun round to face us. He looked shocked and - and scared, no, frightened.

"Stop it!" it was Pierre - or Smith, I can never tell the difference, but even as I was wondering which was which, he turned, thumped the other, then in the shaking light of his torch, ran up the stone stairs.

Smith-or-Pierre gave a melodramatic shriek and ran after him, meanwhile Sketchley was gibbering something clutching his headphones to his ears. "Is it recording?" he virtually shrieked.

There was chaos, everyone milling about, everyone spooked, someone knocked into a light and it crashed over, sending weird shadows chasing round the vaulted ceiling.

Jess grabbed my arm. "Look at the ichosimeter!"

It was going wild, something was making a sound - inside the walls, and the ichosimeter was registering it, and Sketchley's equipment was recording it!

Someone tripped over a cable and pulled something out of a socket, Sketchley's headphones maybe, and there was a roaring whistling sound, sort of feedback and the sound of distant voices like a not tuned-in radio.

Jess grabbed my hand, I dropped the ichosimeter and we belted up the steps, and dark and wild as it was outside, it wasn't half as scary as being inside.

The film club subset didn't meet again, in fact Jess and I stopped going to the film club at all. We'd meet up with Steve and Hampson, and sometimes we'd begin to talk about the stone tape, but the conversation soon moved on to something else.

A Slipped Disc

Brian Price

'What the hell could I have done with it?' Laura asked herself, looking around the bombsite of a living room where her daughter, Lindsey, was playing. A DVD couldn't just disappear, could it? Particularly not this DVD, which had cost her over a thousand pounds.

It had taken the private investigator many days to get the evidence she needed: evidence that her slimy husband was playing away. He had charged her for every minute of his time, but it was worth it. She could now take Derek to the cleaners in the divorce court, retain custody of their little girl and leave him to shag his tarty secretary until the bitch dumped him – which, Laura was sure, wouldn't take her very long.

Laura had been suspicious of Derek for some time. There was nothing obvious, like lipstick on his collar telling a tale, or long blonde hairs on his shoulders, but his behaviour had changed. He had started to go into work early, keen to get to the office, whereas three months ago he had always dragged himself reluctantly out of the house in the mornings. He often came home late, the hint of a suppressed smirk on his face, claiming, when Laura challenged him, that work had been building up.

Derek had also begun to take more care with his appearance: shaving more thoroughly, investing in a new deodorant and changing his shirt daily. Alarm bells rang for Laura and, when she Googled *ishecheating.com*, she was hardly surprised to find that this was a red flag. His lack of interest in her in the bedroom was another indicator, but that had been going on for some time.

She was scared to confront him without evidence. She knew he was an accomplished liar and also had a temper. So, she dug into her savings account and made an appointment to see a former police officer at Mexton Investigations, a firm which promised a discreet and efficient service in these matters. Shocked as she was by the costs, she hired him to investigate her husband.

Three weeks later, the investigator phoned and invited Laura to call into the office. Nervously, she announced her arrival to the receptionist and was shown into her contact's office.

"I'm afraid it's bad news, Mrs Archer," he said, looking slightly embarrassed. "Your suspicions are correct. Derek has been having an affair. I've been able to get several recordings of him and a young woman engaging in sexual activity. In one case they are in his car and in two others they are in her bedroom. In their haste, they forgot to draw the curtains. The clips are on this DVD, along with shots of them holding hands while entering and leaving her apartment building."

He slipped the DVD into a plain cardboard sleeve and handed it to Laura.

"I'm sorry," he said. "It's always hard when you find out someone's been cheating on you. Please let me know if you need me to do anything else."

"Thank you, Mr Rowse," said Laura. "At the moment, I feel sick with anger, but I'll get back in touch if I need you again. Goodbye."

She left the office in a boiling fury. Should she put this on the internet and shame the pair of them? A nice idea, but probably illegal. Revenge porn, they called it, didn't they? Should she confront him at home and throw him out, assuming, of course, that she could force him to go? Or simply set fire to his suits and his precious collection of football programmes. No. She would take her time, consult a solicitor, and then royally shaft him. And she was damned if he would have anything more than occasional contacts with their daughter.

The problem now, of course, was that she couldn't find the DVD. And, whatever happened, Derek mustn't find it. Telling Lindsey to go and watch Peppa Pig or something, she rummaged through the piles of discarded clothing, upturned the sofa, pulled open drawers, removed cushions from the chairs and even searched the waste bins and the washing machine. No joy. How could she have been so stupid? She was at the point of despair when she heard a puzzled cry from Lindsey.

"Mummy. What's Daddy doing with that lady?"

Revenge

The Water of Life

Fenja Hill

Agnes ran, panting, stumbling over rocks and through undergrowth, trying to ignore the pain in her scratched and bleeding bare feet, her chin tucked into her chest to avoid the worst of the assault. Her skirts caught on brambles, and she reached down with her left hand to tug herself free, right arm raised to try and protect her face. More stones thudded into her back and shoulders, followed by a shower of pebbles that rained down on her already bleeding head.

The whole village was behind her, even the children, who were having great fun, picking up handfuls of small stones and hurling them at the fleeing girl. She briefly wondered if they understood what they were doing. Would they have nightmares later? She couldn't help but hope so.

She ran on, rubbing one hand across her eyes to wipe away the trickling blood that mingled with her tears and had begun to obscure her vision. Too late. By the time she could see where she was going, she was within inches of the boundary wall, and she slammed into it and collapsed on the ground.

There was a roar from the villagers as they pushed closer, and stones rained down even more heavily as Agnes dragged herself to her feet and, with the last of her strength, hauled herself up and over the wall, scrabbling with her bloodied fingertips and toes to find purchase.

She had never been past the village boundary and, if she had, would have used one of the gates rather than climbing over the wall, so she had no idea what to expect on the other side. She hit the ground hard, but there was no time to struggle to her feet, because she immediately began to roll downwards. In the midst of her terror, she recognised that this was a good thing. Curling up as tightly as possible, she allowed her body to descend, scratched and stabbed by trees and bushes, but no longer pursued by those who had, until yesterday, been her friends, neighbours and family.

At the bottom of the slope, she lay still for a long time, allowing her body to rest. If she had run through a gate, they would have followed her, but when they set her loose for the chase, they had made it impossible for her to go in any direction but this one. Now, she understood that the priest had arranged this deliberately, anticipating that she would be trapped against the wall. She should have died there. Well, she hadn't. In spite of her pain, anger was beginning to replace her fear and confusion.

Once she was back on her feet, Agnes made slow and careful progress through the scrubland, until, eventually, she found a track. Turning away from the only home she had ever known, she trudged on.

As she walked, Agnes's anger grew. She felt that she should be most angry with the priest. After all, it was he who had forced himself on her, had held her down and whispered threats about what would happen if she said anything to anyone. God would punish her; it was her own fault for raising such desires in him.

The truth was, though, that she was most angry with her mother, to whom she had run, in tears and pain, as soon as he had released her. She could not believe that God would punish her for being attacked and assaulted like that, and she needed the comfort of her mother's arms. How could she have known that her mother would react by dragging her, screaming and struggling, before the very man who had so recently attacked her, and denouncing her as a liar and a blasphemer.

Anger at the mindless fury of the rest of the village, including the children, burned in her too. At her "trial", she had cried and pleaded, looking to the women especially. She could not, surely, have been the only girl to have suffered at that man's hands. At least a few of the women helping to condemn her must have suffered the same assault. But no-one spoke up for her, no-one would even make eye contact. She hated them all. Cowards.

She walked through the night and, as the sun rose, she saw cottages in the distance. She tried to tidy herself up a little, but knew she still looked ragged and unkempt. She was so hungry. Even if the people here wouldn't allow her to stay, perhaps they would give her a piece of bread.

As she approached the first cottage, she heard shouting, and turned to see a group of men, further down the track, waving their arms and yelling at her. They clearly wanted her to go away, but she was so tired and so hungry and thirsty; surely, they could spare her a crust before she continued on her way? She walked towards them; hands outstretched in supplication. To her surprise, they backed away. Were they afraid of her?

And then she saw them. Saw the reason for the men's reaction and realised that they were not afraid of her, but of what would happen to her if she came closer. Beside the track, covered roughly in blankets, lay the bodies. Adults and children, row upon row, awaiting a decent burial. It was only now that she noticed the shovels in the hands of the men. They had been on their way to bury their dead when she appeared.

Of course, she had heard tales of the terrible sickness sweeping the villages, but Wellven had remained cut off and safe. Nobody had left the village for some time, other than to tend the fields. Their water came from their own well, and not from the streams that ran from one village to another, and, so far, nobody had become sick.

Panicked, Agnes turned to leave, intending to run back in the direction from which she had come. She spun round too quickly however, and tripped, arms waving wildly, as she tried to prevent the inevitable. It wasn't possible. She landed heavily on the nearest body, with a sound that would stay with her forever, and rolled slightly, coming face to face with another. Desperately attempting to extricate herself, she only made things worse, and now she was screaming.

The men with the shovels came towards her, having decided that there was no longer any point in trying to protect her. They hauled her up and calmed her, offering her cool water and leading her away to sit on a bench under a tree. Their kindness, after the last few days, was a balm. Agnes sat quietly and watched, as they crossed to the far side of the track and began preparing the graves. As they worked, she saw one off them stumble and fall, clutching his stomach. She heard him retching, and she turned away. She could not stay here. Death was everywhere. Nor could she return to her home, but for now, she would retreat along the track she had arrived on, and sit in the sunshine, away from the stench of death.

Curled up on the grass, Agnes allowed herself to doze, only waking as the sun began to set. She had slept for hours. Her mind turned immediately to the priest, to her mother and to the friends and neighbours who had cast her out. Would, in fact, have killed her, if she had not escaped. It was their fault that she was here, torn and bruised, with nowhere to go and no-one to turn to. Her anger burned so deeply that she thought she could feel it as a physical thing in her gut, rolling and churning. Moments later, she understood that it was not her anger that had caused those feelings, as she vomited with such force that her whole body trembled. She laid her head on the ground, breathing deeply to try and stop the shaking, but nothing helped.

Struggling to her feet, Agnes realised that, while the vomiting seemed to have stopped for a moment, something far worse was about to happen. Crouching, she managed to drag her tattered skirts out of the way before her bowels opened and the whole of her insides seemed to gush out.

She could no longer pretend not to understand what was happening. Tears streamed down her face and her body shook, not only with the disease, but with rage. That man, who the whole village practically worshipped, had done this to her, with his unholy desires. It should be he, not her, who suffered like this. And the others, they were as bad. She was certain that there were women in the village who knew she was telling the truth, but they had come with their children and stoned her, chased her from her safe home into this hell.

She would teach them.

It took a long time for Agnes to reach her village, staggering and stumbling along the track in the dark; stopping frequently to empty her body one way or the other, until she felt she would turn inside out with the effort and pain. She reached a gate just before dawn, and silently let herself in. Very soon, people would be up and about, tending the sheep, working in the fields, living their lives, but for now, everything was still. Her breath came in short gasps now, and she was desperately thirsty, but there was no time for that. Her legs gave way, and she dropped to her knees.

Agnes crawled slowly towards the well. She paused beside it, and with one final effort, pulled herself up and leaned over, peering down into the depths. She struggled to lift her right leg up onto the low wall, but after that it was easy. Leaning forward and lifting her other foot from the ground was all it took. She smiled as she tumbled into the darkness.

Payback

Brian Price

Sally never failed at anything she set her mind to. But she did this time and it was Pete's fault. If he hadn't come home early from the pub and found her, she would have succeeded at suicide as well. Life wasn't perfect but she had a home, a partner, and was looking forward to starting a family. Until recently, she enjoyed her career, doing a job she was proud of. But a new manager, with the humanity of a chainsaw, had undermined her so much that she felt a failure at everything.

Lying in a hospital bed, a drip in her arm and her stomach sore from the gastric lavage, which washed out the paracetamol before it could wreck her liver, she thought back over the previous six months. The sleepless nights, the exhaustion, the drinking, the rows with her partner – all these she blamed on one person. Kelly Thornbury. The woman who had wrecked her life by making her workplace intolerable.

Nothing she could do was good enough for Kelly. Her workload had increased enormously and her supervision meetings with Kelly consisted of a barrage of criticisms and unreasonable demands. She had to work at home during weekends, just to keep up. Sally was a professional person, capable of making her own judgements and managing her commitments. But, since Kelly had arrived, she had been belittled, undermined and insulted. Kelly's bullying wasn't confined to Sally. Her colleagues had suffered in the same way and several had left their jobs as a result. It was the organisation's culture, of which Kelly was a part, which drove them away.

Sally deeply regretted giving in to her despair and the pain it had caused Pete and her parents. She realised that the prompt actions of the paramedics and doctors had given her a second chance, one she would not waste. The only thing to do was to fight back. And she bloody well would.

The days off while she recovered gave her time to plan. For the first time in months, she was away from work and had time to think. She was determined to pay Kelly back for the misery which she had caused her and her colleagues. Sally wasn't a violent person but she was clever. Maybe there were better ways of getting revenge than through physical confrontation?

Sally spent hours devising ways of humiliating, or otherwise harming, Kelly, from letting down her tyres to poisoning her coffee. The more fanciful and illegal ideas she quickly discounted, as well as those which could throw suspicion on herself. Eventually, she settled on a couple of projects which carried a slight risk but which would be highly satisfying to carry out. She waited until she was about to return to work before starting her campaign. She wanted to see the results of her efforts.

Sally knew where Kelly lived and what her regular movements between the office and home were. She also knew the registration number of Kelly's black Ford Focus. It was easy to hire an identical model for the day, from a firm a couple of dozen miles away. Using painted cardboard and black insulating tape, cut to the appropriate sizes, she made copies of Kelly's number plates. Pulling into a side road not far from the office, and checking that no-one was watching, she fixed the copied plates to the hired car, her hands shaking. They wouldn't fool a police officer but, from a distance, they could pass for genuine. Shortly before Kelly was due to leave the office for home, Sally pulled out of the side road and headed along the route Kelly would take.

As she approached the only functioning speed camera in town her heart went into overdrive and her hands on the wheel became slippery with sweat. Looking around for parked police cars – or possible unmarked ones – she was relieved to see that there were no suspicious vehicles in sight. Just before she reached the camera, she put her foot down, reaching 42 mph as she passed the yellow box, which flashed obligingly.

Sweat pouring from her, and her heart thumping almost loud enough to hear above the engine, she pulled into the next available side road. She removed the false plates and sat in the car, trembling, for ten minutes. Gradually, her terror gave way to a feeling of exultation. Kelly would get a speeding ticket and points on her licence, while she had got away with it. For the first time ever, she felt she had exerted some power over her nemesis and it felt good. So good that she couldn't wait to launch the next phase.

Returning to work, with Kelly's speeding ticket no doubt in the post, Sally underwent an intrusive back-to-work interview. She had to convince Lorna Brake, Kelly's boss and the chief executive of the organisation, that she was fit to return. She didn't dare say why she had overdosed but made up a story about having a blinding headache and accidentally taking too many tablets, because of the confusion it had caused. She knew that, if she blamed Kelly's management style for her suicide attempt, she would be accused of gross misconduct and sacked. Lorna's manner was as sympathetic as a rat trap and all she said was 'Don't make that mistake again.' She countersigned the form on which Sally stated that she felt fit to return and dismissed her without so much as a "Welcome back."

***

Sally's organisation was set up to help vulnerable people in the community, be they homeless, substance abusers, gamblers, victims of domestic violence or in chronic debt. Originally part of the local authority, the organisation had been privatised as a community interest company. Sally, and most of her colleagues, cared deeply about their clients, often putting in hours of unpaid overtime to support them. The managers had different attitudes, however, being driven by targets and statistics rather than the human needs of the people they were supposed to support. They had no training in the fields relevant to the clients yet criticised the way in which those actually doing the work performed. Since privatisation, Lorna had replaced a service ethos with a bullying culture. The four managers followed her lead in squeezing every last drop of productivity out of the staff and anyone complaining was threatened with disciplinary action. Salaries had been cut and working hours extended. Most of the staff were desperate to leave but opportunities for people with their skills, in that part of the East Midlands, were rare.

Many of the organisation's clients had problems with alcohol and were put on various treatment regimes. During a training day, Sally had found out about Antabuse, a drug given to alcoholics which produces an adverse reaction should they drink anything with alcohol in it. Sally discovered that Antabuse can be purchased from overseas sites, via the Internet, and she determined to acquire some.

***

Two days after returning to work, Sally had her first supervision meeting. Kelly had always treated Sally with an air of superiority but this time she was downright aggressive, making it clear that Sally would be given no special treatment following her illness. She would be expected to clear her backlog of work without delay. Sally didn't dare to point out the unreasonableness of Kelly's attitude but secretly rejoiced. The ticket's arrived! she thought.

***

Three weeks later, Christmas gatherings were taking place and the Antabuse Sally ordered had arrived. Staff were allowed an extra half hour for lunch to celebrate and most of them went to a local restaurant for a hurried Christmas meal – with no alcohol permitted if they were returning to work. The managers had an evening meal planned and this gave Sally her opportunity. Kelly was an avid coffee drinker, taking it black, sweet and strong. While she was in the toilet, and everyone else was absorbed in completing paperwork before the Christmas break, Sally struck. On the pretext of dropping some expenses sheets on her desk, she stirred two ground-up Antabuse tablets into Kelly's coffee. She wouldn't be around when they took effect, but she could imagine the results at the managers' dinner that evening.

***

The Swanley Hotel was famous for its food, but was not so expensive that the cost of the managers' meals couldn't be massaged through the company's expenses system. The group took their places at the table, anticipating a fine meal and plenty to drink, all on the company's account. Presiding over her minions, Lorna was every inch the Queen Bee, with her Gucci handbag prominently displayed on the table and an expensive dress straining to contain her chest. Once the waiter had poured champagne, she raised her glass 'To another profitable year,' she toasted. Her colleagues joined in the salute, drained their glasses and settled down to consider the menu.

A few minutes later, Kelly began to feel ill. She broke out in a sweat, started to tremble and lurched to her feet in a frantic attempt to reach the toilets. Unfortunately for her, and for her colleagues, she didn't make it. The full effects of the wine, combined with the Antabuse, kicked in and a torrent of vomit poured from Kelly's mouth, filling Lorna's cleavage and soaking her precious bag. Kelly dashed for the Ladies, trailing vomit behind her, while waiters flapped ineffectually at the pool of sick on the table. Lorna was incandescent and stormed off to confront Kelly, who was hunched over a toilet bowl as her body tried to clear the last of the alcohol from her system.

"You stupid cow," snarled Lorna, no trace of sympathy in her manner. "You'll pay for cleaning this dress and replacing my handbag. I'll discuss your behaviour in the office on Monday."

Reeking with the smell of sick, Lorna stalked out of the restaurant, grabbing a full bottle of wine on the way. Her three remaining colleagues, whose appetites had vanished, also left, promising that the company would cover the restaurant's cleaning costs. Kelly eventually emerged from the toilets, weak and wobbly, and slunk to her car without looking at the staff or the horrified customers. She didn't notice Sally in the corner of the hotel car park, making a call on her mobile.

As Kelly's car pulled out of the car park, somewhat erratically, the blue and red lights of a police car ordering her to stop appeared in her mirror. She knew she wouldn't fail a breath test but the indignity of being stopped and tested, while reeking of vomit, made a ghastly evening even worse. She had never felt so miserable in her life.

Best Served Cold

Lois Elsden

I'm not a vengeful person at all; I don't mean I can forgive and forget... I forgive, but I have the sort of memory that can't forget. However, I have never been one to say 'serves him/her right' or to try and seek a way of getting my revenge on anyone! I might be very cross, and I might tell them so, but I would never do anything to deliberately 'pay back' anyone for a wrong they did me.

The Elsden family in general, are not like that. I won't give any examples from more recent times but will tell you a story about my dad, Donald when he was really quite young, probably nine or ten in about 1928-29. He was living with his parents and brother and sister in a pub in Cambridge called the Portland Arms Hotel. Donald was quite a mischievous boy, he got up to all sorts of tricks and was not always caught or found out. Reuben and Maud, his parents, were so modern in the way they brought up their children; they were strict but fair, and their children adored them and could talk to them about anything in a way which we arrogantly think is 'modern'. Donald, Sid and Joan even called their parents by their names, rather than Mum and Dad.

When they were living in the Portland, they had a miserable neighbour, whose name I don't know but I'll call Mrs Brown. One day, Mrs Brown came to the pub and told Maudie that Donald had broken one of her windows. In actual fact, Donald had been out all day with his friend Sammy. Reuben came home from playing golf with his friends at the Gog Magog Golf Club, and Maudie told him about Donald breaking Mrs Brown's window.

Reuben went up to Donald's room, and asked him about it. Donald denied it, but Rue believed Mrs Brown, and thought Donald was not telling the truth. This was the 1920's don't forget, so Reuben put Donald across his knee and gave him the slipper. Donald was a pragmatic boy and thought to himself that he had done plenty of naughty things which Reuben didn't know about so he might as well accept the punishment for something he hadn't done rather than making a fuss and calling Mrs Brown a liar.

Later, Reuben found out that Donald had been away with Sammy for the day and couldn't possibly have broken the window. Rue was distraught! He'd punished his boy for something he hadn't done, and what was worse, he had not believed him when he was telling the truth! He was extremely upset and apologised to Donald - who actually hadn't been that bothered about being slippered. However, the sight of Rue being so upset really upset Donald in turn. How dare Mrs Brown say such a thing! How dare she accuse him of something he hadn't done which ended up with his own father being almost in tears?

Now, here in the story is where the proverb *'revenge is a dish best served cold'* comes into play. Donald was a crack shot with a catapult; he was also a keen fisherman and in those days lines were weighted with lead shot, tiny balls of lead. A month after the slippering incident, Donald took his catapult, carefully positioned himself and put a small lead fishing weight through one of Mrs Brown's window panes. It would have made a tiny hole, but the pane would need replacing. A few days later, maybe a week or two, he did it again with another, different window. Over the next few months, he carefully and strategically took out every pane of every window in Mrs Brown's house with his catapult and lead fishing weights... and all because Mrs Brown had really upset his father, Rue.

Of course, I don't approve of that, and I could never be like that, but it does give me some insight into the Elsden psyche... and I am an Elsden!

Donald

In the Bag

Macaque

He heard the door to the stairwell bang back against the wall, and the older boys' voices echoed against the stark breeze blocks. Instantly he was on his feet, pushing his books neatly to the side of his desk, pushing the chair squarely underneath, then he unlocked his locker, climbed expertly inside, and pushed the catch down with his thumb.

He heard the study door open with a heavy kick, and he cowered in the dark, cramped space, not daring to peek through the narrow slit of light at the edge of the door.

"Where is he?" said a loud, familiar voice.

"I don't know, he didn't come -" There was the sound of a scuffle and a chair falling backwards.

"Where," the voice asked, more menacingly, "is he?"

Inside the locker, Wiggy cringed like an exposed mollusc and closed his eyes.

"I said I don't know!" his study mate said in a small but defiant voice, but he must have glanced or nodded or pointed towards the locker because the silence that followed seemed conspiratorial, and he could sense the proximity of the sixth formers on the other side of the door.

"Right, get on with your work, scum. What's this you're reading? Read it aloud."

Wiggy heard Ed's voice again, reading from *To Kill a Mocking Bird*, and wondered what was going to happen next. He heard the study door close.

"'Jem was twelve. He was difficult to live with, inconsistent, moody. His appetite was appalling, and he told me so many times to stop pestering him I consulted Atticus'" read his pal, stiltingly; he must have been glancing up from the page to see what the older boys were doing.

Vickerstaff took out a canister of lighter gas from his jacket pocket, removed the cap, and aimed the nozzle through the gap in the locker door. His two goons grinned encouragement.

"'This change in Jem had come about in the last two weeks. Mrs Dubose was not cold in her grave -'"

"Hey!" shouted Wiggy as he smelled the gas, "Hey! What are you doing?"

"Shut up, scum!" said Vickerstaff, "You got it coming, you little worm."

Wiggy thumbed the latch back open and pushed against the door, but one of the boys had his knee and shoulder pressing against the outside.

"Hey!" coughed Wiggy, his eyes watering on account of the gas.

The canister ran out, and Vickerstaff pumped the nozzle a few times, then threw it into the junior boys' bin. They would have to smuggle it out, thought Ed, or there would be trouble.

"Now then, you ever heard of Guy Fawkes, you miserable scumbag?" Vickerstaff said to the locker, fishing in his pocket for the Zippo.

"Go on, Vick!" said one of his goons, and they all laughed.

"'The beginning of that summer boded well: Jem could do as he pleased - '" There was a boom, a scream, a flash of blue light followed by a wisp of yellow flame, and the locker door burst open, and a small boy, coughing and crying and smoking a little tumbled out onto the floor at the sixth formers' feet.

Vickerstaff hauled the poor wretch up, shook him until he was standing squarely and staring back at him with laughable indignation, then he smoothed his hair, dusted his shoulders, elbows and lapels, and said: "You owe me a can of gas, scum." Then the three of them left, laughing their way up the corridor.

"You ok?" asked Eddie.

"No thanks to you," replied Wiggy bitterly. There was a whining in his ears and the smell of gas and burnt hair in his nostrils. Some of the hair on the left side of his head had melted into odd clumps, and his jacket was noticeably singed in places. "Mum's going to kill me. Those bastards! I'll get even with them if it's the last thing I do."

As always, the junior boys did their best to avoid Vickerstaff and his 'droogs' as he called them after reading *A Clockwork Orange*. Which English master's bright idea it had been to study that book Wiggy would have loved to have known. Wiggy stayed with groups of friends at break times and between classes, and went to the library for study periods whenever possible. But messages kept reaching him – 'Vick says "don't forget"', 'Vick says you owe him', 'Vick says you've got the weekend – Monday morning, or else.'

"I think you should just get him the can, Wigs," said Eddy, more than once. "Can't be that expensive, and there's only a slim chance you could get caught with it before you hand it over. Doesn't mean he's won." He even offered to split the cost.

Wiggy thought about it, then said, "You know, you're right. We'll get him the can. Ask everyone to chip in, will you? See how much we can get."

On Thursday, after games, the sixth formers were all in the showers, whipping whoever they could with wet towels and hollering like baboons. With sentries posted, Wiggy dashed into Vickerstaff's study and removed his distinctive satchel with *The Sex Pistols*, *Iron Maiden* and *Metallica* scrawled over it in black biro. On the way home, he waited outside the shop on Eastman Street until he spied a likely accomplice. All he had to do now was stay safely out of the bully's reach for another twenty-four hours.

When the caretaker locked up on Friday evening, he found a satchel covered in biro graffiti left in a corner of the Senior bike shed. He picked it up and glanced inside, uttered an exclamation of surprise, then took it to the headmaster.

"Where's my gas can, you miserable little scumbag, I'm nearly out. Time's up, come on. Hand it over, or else."

"Vickerstaff, my office, now, please." The headmaster's voice was stern. With a dark look, the senior boy let go of Wiggy and proceeded in the master's wake.

"Mr Timms found your satchel on Friday evening," said the headmaster, placing the bag on his desk.

"My bag went missing last week - "

"Silence," continued the headmaster. "When Mr Timms opened the bag to ascertain ownership," the headmaster opened the flap on the satchel now, "he was most distressed at the contents." He brought out the items as he spoke. "One canister of lighter fuel; one half consumed packet of cigarettes; one box of condoms, two remaining, and these...magazines. I didn't realise your German was quite that proficient, Vickerstaff, or perhaps you just look at the pictures. Either way, your career at this school has come to a premature end. You are dismissed."

Next

; o o o o o o ?

Customer Service

Brian Price

"Can I help you?" the young assistant asked, as the middle-aged woman plonked a plastic bag on the counter before her.

"Yes please. I'd like to return this cardigan."

"Certainly, madam. Is there anything wrong with it?"

"I just didn't like the colour when I got it home. It looked different in daylight." She waved at the shop's bright LED lights. "These things make everything look funny."

The assistant smiled sympathetically.

"That's fine. When did you buy it?"

"Only a few days ago. Well within your return period."

"Of course. May I see the receipt?"

"I don't have it. I never keep those things. Too much clutter."

"Oh dear. I'm afraid we can't offer a refund without a receipt. Store policy. I'm sorry."

"But that's ridiculous. Are you suggesting I stole it? It's in one of your bags."

"No, madam. Of course not. It's just our rule. Do you, by any chance, have a credit card receipt or a statement? That would do as proof of purchase."

"No, I don't, young lady. I paid cash. Four twenty-pound notes and a ten-pound one. I had a pound in change. I suppose you'll be asking me for the serial numbers next."

"No, of course not. Is there, perhaps, something else in the store you would like to exchange it for? I think the manager would be able to authorise that."

"No, there isn't. I've seen nothing else like it. And I think you'd better get the manager out here right now. I will not be treated in this way. I've been shopping here for many years and expect better service than this."

The assistant called over a smartly dressed older woman and muttered briefly in her ear, before attending to another customer. Her colleague walked briskly over to the woman at the counter and smiled.

"Good morning, madam. I'm Estelle, the manager, and I understand you wish to return an item without a receipt."

"Yes, I do. And that young girl was extremely unhelpful."

"I'm afraid my colleague was only following company policy. Staff are not allowed to issue a refund without a receipt."

She pointed to a notice on the wall advising customers to retain receipts in case they wished to return items.

"Are you sure there is nothing else you would like?"

"I've already told her. No. It's my money I want. And an apology for this treatment."

The manager paused for a moment, clearly trying to decide on the best way of getting rid of this troublesome customer.

"All right. I think I can make an exception on this one occasion, as long as it's still a stock item."

Grumpily, the customer passed over the bag. The manager opened it, examined the contents and smiled slightly.

"I'm sorry, madam. We will not be able to refund you after all."

"Why on earth not? You said you would."

"Yes, but that cardigan came from Marks and Spencer. This is Next."

Mr Harland
Lois Elsden

We used to call them doorknob lessons, back in the olden days when teaching was all about opening young minds, and going off-piste as the whim took us. Lesson prep was somewhat sketchy in many senses, and inspiration might strike as your hand lighted on the door handle of the classroom. Think L. P. Hartley, think of the past as a very foreign country, when things we did then would be unrecognisable today.

2LE were not only my form, they were also my favourite form, I think they were probably my favourite class of all time. I had such fun teaching them, and apparently as some have recently told me, they had fun too.

To be honest, I'd had a rather late night, the pub closed and we drifted into town to the Lamplight. It was a dodgy club which played great music between performances from young ladies who took their clothes off. Yes, it was that sort of dodgy. The previous night, we'd left the Lamplight, and heading back to where we were staying, noticed that the West Indian Club was still open and still serving, so... Well, it was somewhat late when my head hit the pillow on the couch at my friend's flat where I was crashing.

So, that morning, I'd already seen 2LE first thing when I took the register, but I greeted them again and decided they could spend the lesson writing a story. First, we'd talk about what they might write and I got them to bring their chairs to the front and they huddled round me, knowing the longer they sat here being sociable and chatting, the less actual work they would do.

I'm sure they realised I was easily sidetracked from whatever scrappy plan I had for the lesson. They must have known that if they got me telling some tale, I'd waffle on for ages, with any luck until the bell rang.

"You're looking a bit pale, miss!" said Keith, cheekily, and there were a few giggles.

"Well, you'd look a bit pale if you'd seen what I saw first thing!" I exclaimed and there was outright laughter because Keith's parents had come from Tobago to work in the mills, when there were mills in Oldham.

I had to regain ground, I wasn't on top form, to be honest.

"You know I always come into school really early because I live over the other side of Manchester?" and they all nodded, settling down for me going on and them not having to do anything. "Well, for some reason, I misread the time, and got to the bus station earlier than usual, and as there was an Oldham bus already in, I got on and arrived before the cleaners."

"So did you have a kip in the staffroom?" Steve asked.

"No, I did not, Stephen, but it's funny you should say that…" I glanced round as if checking we were alone, and craned my head to look at the window in the door. "Look I shouldn't really be telling you this, but I had a real shock!"

"You do still look a bit pale, miss," Sajida said kindly.

"Well," I glanced at the window in the door again, and they all looked too. "You mustn't mention this outside the classroom…" they shuffled their chairs closer. "You see, when I arrived and went into the staffroom, there was Mr Harland stretched out on the seats."

There were some giggles and someone asked if he'd slept the night there. They knew Niall Harland was a friend of mine and so were expecting some story about him.

"Worse than that - no, I can't tell you!" and I looked at the window in the door again.

Of course they wanted to know, and with apparent reluctance, I told them. They mustn't tell anyone, it was absolutely secret for the good of the school, it was being hushed up… but, he had been murdered!

There was a shocked silence, and then Jessica gave a nervous giggle.

"Good story, miss," she said.

"Was there blood everywhere?" asked Haroon in a low voice, and juvenile ghoulishness overcame them and there were more nervous giggles.

"No, thank goodness, no, someone had strangled him with a cheese wire, do you know what one of them is?"

Honestly, this story was becoming more preposterous but I managed to keep a straight face, as I involved Paul Stevens and Tony Jones, the two chunky PE teachers, in removing the body in Arthur McVay's camper van.

"But why? Why did they kill him?"

"Well, you know as soon as we teachers arrive in the staffroom, we have to have coffee, and we each bring our own jar, but Mr Harland was always running out and would "borrow" someone else's! I can't tell you who, except it wasn't me, but someone was so fed up they… Well, you can guess!"

There was a stunned silence.

It was the 80's and kids were more gullible then, but even so, as I looked round at their wide-eyed faces, I really couldn't believe that -

"Hang about!" Nusreen, who was usually very quiet, suddenly spoke. "I saw Mr Harland this morning, he was in his office having a fag!"

And someone else piped up that they'd seen him coming out of the headmistress's office.

"But that wasn't him, that was his twin brother who used to work in Timbuktu! He was a teacher out there, and came home last week and the head quickly rang him to come in and take over Mr Harland's job to avoid a scandal!"

Timbuktu - I'd used the most ridiculous sounding place I could think of.

"His brother is Mr Lyle Harland, Niall's twin!"

They sat in silence staring at me, eyes wide.

So, what happened next in this ridiculous tale?

The door unexpectedly opened and Niall, Mr Harland, popped his head in. There was a collective intake of breath as the kids stared, pop-eyed at him.

"Everything alright, Miss Elsden?" Niall asked into the silence.

"Fine, thanks, Lyle - oh I mean, Niall, I mean Mr Harland!" I stuttered.

"Well done, 2LE, excellent behaviour!" Niall gave them a friendly wink, and there was another big gasp as he shut the door firmly.

"Right, ok, class, back to your places, books out! I want you to use my story and write about what happened next!"

They picked up their chairs and began to mutter and chatter quietly as they went back to their desks.

"Miss Elsden, that story is actually a joke, isn't it?" Jessica the clever girl said.

"Well, what do you think? Come on everyone, you have twenty minutes to write about what happened next, and you can finish it off for homework!"

Years later at a school reunion for staff and students, I heard people - some who I hadn't even taught, talking about the murder in the staffroom. Niall nudged me.

"Apparently I'm actually my twin brother Lyle," he laughed. "Whatever next?!"

Oxford, 1920

Macaque

    It was a gloriously green evening in the key of G minor, legato, pianissimo. An arpeggio of wings traversed the sky, geese probably, far off, the sultry air swallowing their klaxon calls. Siegfried stood smoking on the terrace, a brown thread tendrilling from one of his waistcoat buttons like the wiry stalks of grass interrupting the paving stones. The scent of his expensive tobacco mingled with the orchestration of aromas from the garden: bass notes of oak, strings of sweet citrus, a fanfare of heady honey from the trumpet bowls in the borders. Such a perfectly blue-green evening, thought Siegfried. He turned at the sound of footsteps, exhaling a compliment of blue-grey smoke.
    "Sass! Well, whatever next!"
    "Oh, woe is me, here among the petals of dusk, owing nothing to the lightness of their touch."
    "It's good to see you, old man," said Wilfred. He transferred the brandy bowl to his left hand and indicated Siegfried's cigarillo subtly with his right. "I don't suppose -"
    "Why is it always when I've been to the emporium? You're never this quick to ask for a Woodbine." He puffed in mock irritation, but fished out his case and lighter and handed them to the younger man. "How have you been?" he asked, once more gazing the length of the garden at the penumbra of empty sky. "How are the dreams?"
    "They come and go," said Wilfred, inhaling deeply, and handing back the silver case. Siegfried fluttered his fingers, and Wilfred surrendered the lighter, too.
    "And you think you can tell the difference?"
    "I'm starting to, yes. I was just saying to Rupert the other day," he paused to draw on the cigarillo, "exquisite!" he remarked.
    "How is The Babbling Brooke?"
    "You know he doesn't like being called that. He doesn't deserve it either."
    "Well, opinions remain personal, at least, whatever the political climate." Siegfried smiled and stepped down onto the lawn.

    The interior of the garden was plush and sophisticated. The cases were mahogany, like the tables, and the books they housed were calf-bound and gilded. The expensive smoke roiled in the air above them like sea snakes, and the leather of the Chesterfields was a deep sea-green.

"And what about me?"

"I think Owing suits you down to your lowly Welsh boots."

"Lowly?"

The older man raised an eyebrow that somehow took in all the opulent surroundings with only a little help from a supercilious eye.

"Point taken. But, then, nothing ever fitted a person so perfectly as Sass does you," he rejoined.

"Quite. And that's my point. A Man can only be what he is."

"Then why do you support the Labour movement?"

Sass laughed now. "Oh, to see the world through such still-innocent eyes! Here, have another before you depart. I'll light it for you."

"Thanks." Smoke darkened the shrinking corners of the room. "I wish I could visit more often. I want to discuss your work."

"I wish you weren't dead," he said, the words leaving his lips as he woke.

Breaking the Silence

Fenja Hill

Every time the voice rang out, Teddy jumped, and every time, he told himself not to be so silly. It was the silence that did it. Nobody in the queue was speaking, everyone was focused on trying to look relaxed. Perhaps they were trying to remember what they were supposed to say. They all knew what would happen if they messed up. Instead of standing together in the queue, Toby's little gang were spaced out between the others, as a reminder; not that anyone needed one. Jason and Sue had been talking for a while, but as they got closer to the front of the queue, their voices dropped to whispers, and eventually stopped altogether.

"Next!"

He jumped again and then tried to pretend he hadn't; not that anyone was looking, they were all too busy looking cool and unconcerned. He shuffled forward as Lily went through the door. The worst of it was, they were sending everyone out from the other side, so no-one who was still waiting got to see or speak to them. Would that be better or worse? Was his imagination worse than the eventual reality would be? At first, he had tried to time how long each person was in there, counting the seconds under his breath, looking for someone who was in there longer than the others. The trouble was, every time the voice shouted, he lost track and forgot all the numbers he was trying to keep in his head. He thought perhaps that Sam had been in there the longest, but he had a stutter, so that was hardly surprising. Daisy was hardly in there any time at all, and he had wondered about that, which meant he was distracted and forgot to count for Jess. In the end, he'd given up with the counting. It didn't matter anyway. Even if someone told them everything, they would probably question everyone else, so that no-one knew who it was; or in case they were making it up.

Teddy's biggest worry was that he had never been able to tell lies. His face went scarlet, he couldn't get his words out and he would often start to cry. He'd spent yesterday evening practicing in front of the bathroom mirror, trying to think of everything they might ask. How much did they know? Nothing, really. They just thought it was odd that Alice had disappeared from her own birthday party and none of the kids who'd been there had seen anything. Teddy hadn't seen anything, so he could safely say that without going scarlet and stumbling over his words. But what if they phrased it differently? There were questions Teddy would not want to answer. He'd started a list:

"Did you know someone had threatened to drown Alice's gerbil?"
"Do you know how Alice's party dress got torn?"
"Have you ever seen anyone bullying Alice?"
And the worst possible question. "Do you know where Alice is now?"

There was only one question he would be happy to answer, and that was, "Teddy, did you hurt Alice?" And he could say truthfully, that of course he hadn't, he had liked her. But he wouldn't add that he was too much of a coward to stand up for her when others hurt her, because he knew what it was like to be that person, and he never wanted to be in that position again.

"Next!"

This time Teddy had been so wrapped up in his thoughts, that he thought he'd die of fright. The line shuffled forward and he took deep breaths, trying desperately to calm himself.

They'd all gone to the party, because Alice had a trampoline and a zip-wire in her enormous garden, and a pond with frogs, and they knew the food would be great because her parents were loaded. That had a lot to do with the bullying; the other kids were jealous. Of course, Alice hadn't told her parents about it; you just didn't. If you were bullied, you dealt with it, or you didn't deal with it, but you absolutely did not get adults involved. Teddy's parents and teachers had no idea of the torment he had experienced until Alice came along. Now, it was as if none of that had ever happened. The kids in his class talked to him, no-one stuck a foot out as he walked past their desk, no-one accidentally knocked his plate onto the floor at lunch; he was just another kid in the class. So, Alice's parents had invited the whole class to her party, assuming they would all be her friends. After all, she was pretty and bright; why wouldn't she have lots of friends?

"Next!" Teddy looked up and realised there were only two more kids before him. His heart was pounding; he thought he was going to pass out; he needed to sit down. Instead, he reached out and put his hand on the wall next to him, resting his weight on it. Toby, standing behind him, asked if he was okay. His tone was not comforting, there was a definite edge to it, and Teddy knew what that meant.

Pulling himself together, Teddy stood up straight and turned, forcing a smile.

"Yeah, I'm just starving. Wish they'd hand out sandwiches or something." He laughed and Toby laughed too, but that didn't necessarily mean he was convinced.

The line moved forward as Ella went through the door. Now, there was only Adil, and then it would be Teddy's turn.

Teddy breathed slowly, counting his breaths and focusing on nothing else. He was only a few feet from the door, but he didn't even hear the next call. Everything was about his breath.

He was jerked out of his reverie by a sharp jab in his back. It was his turn and he hadn't even heard the shout. Toby made sure he moved though, shoving him again. He stepped forward and passed through the door. Somebody closed it quietly, behind him.

There was a table at the far side of the room, with two men sitting at it. There was also a chair, to one side, where a woman sat. One of the men introduced himself as a police officer and the other explained that he was a social worker, here in the place of parents. Teddy suspected that all the parents had agreed to this because each of them thought that, if they refused, the police would think their son or daughter was hiding something. The woman was the school counsellor. Teddy recognised her, although he'd never had any reason to speak to her.

The policeman gestured towards a lonely chair in the centre of the room and asked Teddy if he'd like to sit down. What he wanted, was to fall down. He wanted to cry. He wanted to be sick. He wanted to run from the room. Instead, he sat down.

There was a pause before the policeman spoke again, staring straight through Teddy's eyes, into his soul.

"Teddy, we just need to ask you a few questions. Can you start by telling us…"

Teddy didn't hear the rest of the question. Here and now, in this room, there was only the policeman, who probably had x-ray eyes and could definitely read Teddy's mind. There were no bullies, no friends, no parents. Teddy thought of Alice's mother, running through the house and garden, calling her daughter's name. He thought of his own parents and how they loved him and often told him what a good, caring boy he was. He thought of Toby and that trick he had, of twisting your arm so far up your back that you thought you would pass out with the pain, while your mouth was stuffed with a glove or the sleeve of a jumper, or a bunch of disgusting tissues, so that all you could do was grunt and try not to vomit.

He thought about Saturday afternoon, when there was a queue to get into the toilet, so he had gone to the bottom of the garden, behind the shed, desperate to pee. The shed was the only place they had been told not to explore, because it was old and shaky, left behind by the previous owners of the house, and would be removed soon, so there was no-one else around. There was a shiny padlock on the door.

He thought of the missing panels he had noticed, at the back of the shed, easily creating a hole that a kid his size could pass through. He was desperate to pee though, so he'd turned away, unzipping as quickly as he could, and sighing with relief.

He thought of the grunting noises he had heard through the flimsy wooden walls, causing him to freeze as he zipped up his trousers, wondering what kind of animal had crawled into the shed to make its nest, and whether it was dangerous.

And he thought of the loud crack he had heard, and the frantic change in pitch and volume of the grunting, followed by indeterminate sounds of banging and rattling, the low voices of Toby and his accomplices and the gradually fading grunts and moans. And silence.

All he could hear now was that silence. It was all he would ever hear, unless he broke it.

Teddy didn't wait for the policeman to finish.

Opening his mouth, and barely whispering, Teddy broke the silence.

1000 Word Limit

Mole Vole and Duck

Lois Elsden

It was great to see the pub full again even though I had to elbow my way to the bar. After the unfortunate events three months ago - poor Albie - it seemed for a while that the Mole Vole and Duck would never open its doors again. Thankfully Big Stu decided retirement bored him and he took it on.

Yes, I know Mole Vole and Duck is a ridiculous name, the previous brewery chose it, thinking it might attract a different clientele. They were wrong; the same old regulars latched onto the bar and ignored all the comical quack quips painted on the beams and lintels. Some pedant kept graffitiing in a comma after 'Mole', not realising that the creature is a Mole Vole. A local with a big voice and a gimlet eye soon put them right.

The pub was redecorated, re-carpeted with durable thick carpets, the weird agricultural artefacts and implements were back hanging from the ceiling, securely attached.

It wasn't long before the regular activities were up and running again: the village book club on a Tuesday morning when it was pretty quiet, a walking group lunched twice a month, a snooker league, ditto darts, a quiz, and loads more. Yes, Big Stu knew a trick or two to keep the place busy.

We're on the edge of a national park and we get plenty of tourists dropping in, some staying on the local campsite, some in local B&B's, and Big Stu has opened a couple of bedrooms upstairs in the pub as well.

It's always pretty quiet on a Sunday so we usually drop in then, sit round the bar and gossip, catch up with the news, and argue over the sports results. It's usually just locals, mostly just regulars, but on this particular night there was a couple who were staying upstairs - not a couple as in being a couple, but two blokes in separate rooms.

I think we all assumed they were mates as they had arrived in the same car, had sat together to eat, and both had Welsh accents. It didn't take long to realise that in fact they must have had a massive row, or had never liked each other, or both. They never spoke to the other, only to us.

"I see the pub was closed for a while," said one of them, I think he was called Carl, but he might have been Curt.

No-one answered him but someone asked what part of Wales he came from, and the conversation moved on, for a while.

"Yeah, I was wondering why the pub had been closed - it's had a great refurb," said Carl, in a bland, non-controversial way.

I reckoned at the time that he already knew, and we agreed afterwards that he must have done, it had hit the national newspapers and been on TV too. There had been a move to change the name, but we were all used to the Mole Vole and Duck by now.

"Bloody disgrace the number of pubs closing, what with the breweries and the taxes and people drinking at home!" Old Tony leaning on the bar took breath to launch into his favourite topic and for once none of us interrupted or tried to divert him, but chimed in with our own views on the bloody disgrace.

"So why did the pub close?" Carl persevered, interrupting Old Tony.

"Are you a journo, or something?" Steve demanded. "Why do you keep going on about it?"

Old Tony kicked Steve's ankle surreptitiously then apologised that his foot had slipped, and announced that the drinks were on him; he'd had a win on the gee-gees, and he'd get in beers all round.

There were shouts of "pint of gin for me!" and "mine's a magnum!" and "bucket of Old Mouldy, Big Stu!" Old Tony even got a couple of pints for nosy Carl and his mate.

This might have been where it went a bit awry as we seemed to knock back our pints and then Carl bought us a wee dram, fair play to him, then someone else - not me, bought another by which time we all thought Carl was a fine fellow, and even more so when he bought more wee drams.

You know what happened next: Carl asked yet again why the pub had closed, and Vince, who no-one really liked anyway, told him.

"It was a normal night -" he started.

"Just like this one!" Steve shouted.

"Shut up Steve! It was a normal night, just like this one, not even a dark and stormy night, and we were all in here, weren't we?" Vince looked round.

We also looked round, and suddenly we were quiet, because yes, we had all been here.

"All here except -"

"Shut up, Steve!"

Carl, it seems, had bought a bottle of Laphroaig and while we were all looking at each other like owls, or ducks, or mole voles, he went round, topped us up.

"Go on, Vince," he said. Looking back on it now, he might as well have said *and you are the weakest link, goodbye!*

"We were all in here, just having a drink, like now, and Albie, god rest his soul, just stood up and thought it would be a great idea to..."

And Vince leapt up, to grab and swing on the ancient and supposedly decorative farm implement hanging above him, just as Albie had four months ago - and just as the supposedly decorative, spiky and very heavy farm implement had detached from its secure fitting and skewered Albie, so the cast iron something-or-another detached from the ceiling. This time, instead of Vince, who had grabbed the vile thing, bringing it down on himself, it was Carl standing gazing up who caught it full in his mush.

Needless to say, it was not only the end of the evening, and the end of the Mole Vole and Duck, it was also the end of Carl.

The Historians

Macaque

I cast off with the same sense of adventure every time. There is something elemental about it, leaving land for a life on water, parting with the acquaintances just made for a period of solitude, replacing solidity with roll and ebb and flow; no journey is ever short enough for the casting-off to be mundane. Untethering the vessel and making that leap to the gunwale, mooring line in hand, you know you are unbound, disconnected, free.

I feel my forebears keenly in this more than any other act; Vikings, Phoenicians, Greeks and Romans, Carthaginians, pirate captains and their imperial adversaries from The Time Before, they all shared this pivotal, alchemical feeling at the start of every voyage. I tell you this because I know you will understand. Any sailor worth his salt, as they say, will know when his boat is untethered. Like an archer can feel without checking when his quiver is empty, or a carter knows when a vagabond has slipped onto the back board, however stealthily. Everything changes; subtly but unmistakably. Everything. Like the difference between wake or sleep, night or day.

Here, the river current pulls us from the bank immediately in a slow and steady arc. I push the tiller wide and guide us carefully past the barques, junks, rowers and cruisers that have gathered at the mooring stakes like horses tied to a rail. I know this stretch of river; I can channel her intent for a few miles, steering with the hand tiller, before any need for sail. This bend below the village has caused a swift current and deep passage that is not present further up. The water here is busy, teeming with small craft as well as larger vessels, but wide enough not to be a danger. People here know me as a merchant of coffee and spices, nothing more. I have little to fear among these folk.

The Flaxen Maiden is an old boat, familiar to many across the wide seas. I bought her from an even more ancient spicer, a man named Aurek who was ready to put to shore one last time and live out his days in a small wooden cottage, his grey beard smouldering with the sputtered embers from his pipe bowl. I refitted her myself, making the necessary changes to carry contraband as well as legal cargo. I had my plans ready, had commissioned the boiler I needed prior to the purchase, so the refit was as quick and inconspicuous as any cosmetic, change-of-hands alterations would normally be. I had my workbenches fitted to fold flush with the panelling in the cabin, and in addition to Aurek's sealed spice containers, I had some open display boxes installed, so that the various aromas will mask any trace of glue and other materials.

    The boiler I mentioned provides heat to the cabin and acts as a stove, but also provides steam to work a press and a bellows. I replaced The Maiden's keel with my own design, shaped like a whale-fluke to be shallower, and also to direct jets of compressed air from the bellows. This is how I navigate further up the river than other vessels my size, often under cover of darkness. Finally, more air-tight compartments have been added in clever little nooks, so that the contraband doesn't smell of coffee and paprika, garlic, chilli, marjoram and nutmeg; that would give the game away in an instant. The Flaxen Maiden does her job well; we are a good team, she and I, and business is booming.

    So, now, to business. We ride swiftly down river, high in the water, and as the current slows to a lazy meander, I hoist the sails and gust out of the estuary, away from the land and the towns and the pleasure craft, out into solitude and safety. Here, I can open up the trestles and set out the work benches, bring out the leather and the vellum and start to cut and to stitch, to press and to bind, making the tomes for the stories I will gather, the histories of The Time Before, transcribed from forgotten libraries, or passed down orally over the generations in remote villages. I will gather all these stories as I trade for my cargo of spices, then return slowly, writing the books that I will sell to the black marketeers to spread the true history of our world, of The Time Before, before the Globelite took power, destroying the libraries and the learning centres, banning any version of the truth other than their own.

    I am one of the Historians, a wanted man in a world that doesn't know what it wants, doesn't know what it came from nor what it is. I have recovered, recorded and returned hundreds of facts about our past to the living descendants of that time before The Change. A little of each book remains with me, a kernel of truth at the centre of each story. Over the years I have forgotten details, but in essence I know much about our past. And what I know is this: we were not always the docile fishers and farmers and tradespeople that we are now. Once we were explorers, inventors, poets and artists and dreamers. I have their poetry, seen copies of their works of art, shared their dreams and explorations. The design for the boiler on The Flaxen Maiden came from The Time Before, along with many other ideas that I dare not yet make a reality. But thanks to The Historians, knowledge is spreading like a rising tide, and one day, we will be poets and inventors and adventurous men once more. The Globelite will not know how to repress us when we shed our sheep's wool and remain docile no longer. One day, everyone will know that feeling of casting off, that freedom of thought and action, leaving the land behind and going where the wind takes you, where your own belief can take you.

Crossed Words

Brian Price

"I did Matilda last week. Then I did Imogen. Yesterday's tramp was too hard, but tonight I'll do Paul."

Peter Jacobs nearly choked on his Twix when he heard the bus passenger in front of him, apparently boasting on his mobile phone.

Peter didn't like travelling by bus. The movements made him feel slightly queasy, and he couldn't read his detective story, but, with strikes on the railway, he had little choice. He hated every minute of the journey, confined in an overcrowded vehicle, with people he found rather unsavoury, and frequently being pushed against, elbowed, and knocked by bags and rucksacks. He was constantly annoyed by tinny music escaping from young people's headphones, and business calls made by people who seemed to have forgotten all about client confidentiality. But he hadn't expected to overhear something like this.

What had he heard, though? Had he eavesdropped on an undiscriminating sexual predator, using a vulgar term for his conquests? Or, could it be a serial killer, boasting to an accomplice or fellow member of some secret murder club? That seemed more credible to him, given the plethora of serial killers in his habitual reading matter. If that was the case, Paul, whoever he may be, was in mortal danger. So, what should he do?

Peter decided to go to the police They would know if anyone called Matilda or Imogen had been killed recently. But what if the killer had made it look like natural causes? The names were a bit archaic, so perhaps the victims were elderly, suffocated in a care home or something. That was it. Find a home where two women had been killed and identify Paul.

The police would need evidence, though. More than just an account of an overheard conversation. A description would help or, even better, a photograph. But Peter didn't have a mobile phone and, anyway, he could hardly stand in front of the suspect and ask him to say "cheese'". He could, though, see a partial reflection of his target in the side window of the bus, particularly when it passed through shaded areas. Peter couldn't draw, but he surreptitiously made notes on the back of an envelope. They would have to do.

After several minutes furtive glancing at the suspect's reflection, as well as the back of his head, Peter came up with a rough description. A white man with greying, longish hair and the beginnings of a bald patch. He had a neat, grey beard, and wore glasses with fairly thick black frames. He looked to be in his fifties and seemed quite thin. He wore a tweed jacket and, Peter noticed when he stood up to get off the bus, grey trousers and brown brogues.

Not much to go on, he thought. It could describe hundreds of people in the town. The police would clearly need something else. Of course, in books the detectives always took DNA samples with those mouth swabs, but he couldn't do that. There was DNA in hair, though, wasn't there? Especially one with a root.

Peter peered closely at the back of the man's neck, hoping that his own reflection wouldn't be spotted. He could easily pull out one of the longer hairs, but that would obviously be noticed, and Peter feared he could end up a victim himself. There were some loose hairs on the back of the man's collar. Perhaps they would do instead. He thought hard about how to collect them. He had no tweezers, like the scientists in the *CSI* programmes. Looking at his notes, he realised that the envelope on which he had written them was the self-sealing type and there was some residual stickiness on the flap, where he had opened it carefully. He tore the flap gently from the rest of the envelope and waited for his opportunity, his heart thumping.

For the rest of Peter's journey, the roads were relatively smooth, so he couldn't "accidentally" fall forward, as the bus went over a bump, and make contact with his target's neck. When his stop appeared, he realised he had one last chance. As he stood up, he stumbled and put his hand out, holding the sticky piece of envelope facing outwards, and pressed it against the suspect's collar.

Apologising profusely, he rushed off the bus and slipped his sample, without examining it, into the rest of the envelope to keep it safe. Five minutes later, he was standing at the police station reception desk, explaining to the civilian receptionist that he had captured the DNA of a serial killer.

"So," began DS Jack Vaughan, facing Peter across the table in an interview room. "You overheard someone claiming he'd killed two people, tried to kill another and was planning to murder a fourth tonight. And, you've got this man's DNA."

"That's right, Detective Sergeant," replied Peter, excitedly. "I got some of his hair." He pulled out the envelope but his face fell when he realised that his attempt had failed. "Oh dear. It didn't work."

"Probably just as well," said the detective. "You can't go around taking bodily samples from people for DNA testing without their consent. It's illegal. Anyway, tell me about these people your suspect is supposed to have killed."

"He killed Matilda and Imogen, tried to kill a tramp and is planning to kill Paul."

DS Vaughan looked thoughtful. "What were his exact words?"

"He said he did the first two, the tramp was too hard and he would do Paul tonight. He was talking on his phone."

The detective smiled. "I can put your mind at rest, Mr Jacobs. Those names are all crossword setters in the Guardian newspaper. He was doing the crosswords, not killing people. But thanks for getting in touch. We always appreciate help from the public. Mind how you go."

As Peter left the station, he muttered quietly to himself. "Strewth. For a while, there, I thought I had a rival. And I can't have that, can I?"

Train

K'Homun Umbrakai

Macaque

I had returned to Karaktaal, my gateway to the northern mountains, searching once more for the phoenix. As I took my evening meal by the fire in the main room of the inn, I overheard a strange word in a hushed conversation. I was learning to get by in the local language, aided by a grounding in schoolboy Latin, but I was by no means fluent. Travelling alone, and in search of the arcane, I was accustomed to letting my senses wander as I ate or drank or waited for a conveyance, always hoping to see or overhear some clue that would help me find another phoenix.

After dinner, when I was the only patron left in the bar-cum-dining room, I asked Otuq, the landlord, what the word was that I had picked up; its roots had sounded like something to do with travelling and a shadow man.

"Ah," growled Otuq in his thick, dark accent, "I believe you would say it in your tongue as 'ghost train'; but be warned, it is not what you think."

"How do you know what I think?" I asked amiably. Like all men in these parts, he had a gruff and brutal countenance, but we had talked at great length for one so wary of strangers, and I liked him.

"It is what everyone thinks," uttered my host.

"I am not everyone," I smiled, taking a meaningful draught from my mug of the local brew.

"Yes, you are," replied Otuq, his black beard parting to reveal his black teeth in what might also have been a smile. "That is what is mean 'everyone'." He chuckled and replenished my mug.

I liked this answer, for its semantics, very much, but it wasn't particularly helpful. "So, what is this K'homun umbrakai, this ghost train?"

"This I cannot say," he said gravely, turning to put the bottle back on its shelf, but as he did so, his dark eyes flicked to the chimney breast behind me.

As I said, I am always on the look out for clues and hints, and I turned, now, to look at the fireplace. There was a grainy sepia photograph of the mountains hanging there, framed and labelled by an early explorer; I had studied it when I arrived and glanced at it from time to time as I had dined and eavesdropped over several evenings. I went and looked at it again; just visible among the snow and trees and rock, was what appeared to be a monastery.

    It took me two days to find a mule guide willing to take me even part of the way to the monastery. These were mountain people, very superstitious and as respectful of traditions as they were resistant to change. Eventually a young man named Ketaq agreed to take me to the edge of the forest for an exorbitant fee. As he secured the money in his belt pouch, I heard him whisper "I pray to the mountain god that you will not be admitted." I looked at him for a minute, but he said nothing further, and avoided my eye until some miles had passed.

    And so we made our way on foot, the mule being a pack animal to carry supplies only, and not for riding. Only as a carcass would I get to sit up there, joked my guide, although he may not have meant it as a joke, in hindsight. Our progress slowed as the snow deepened and the gradient increased. The air was sharp to the lungs and starved of oxygen, so while we walked we made little conversation. At night, when we made camp, I tried to talk to Ketaq, and when he remained silent, which was often, I made sketches of him and the mountains in my notebook.

    On the fifth day, we entered the forest, and the going became a little easier once more. Although not exactly a road nor a track, there was at least a way through the trees, with frosted earth underfoot instead of snow up to the knees. Apart from the sounds of branches flexing and rubbing in the wind above our heads, all was silent and gloomy, including Ketaq. The forest was like no place else on earth that I had ever known. Ketaq wouldn't stop for lunch, so we kept walking, and chewed on salted beef, sharing a flask of warm coffee that he had made before smothering the camp fire that morning.

    At about three o'clock in the afternoon, the forest began to thin and lighten, traces of snow could be seen beneath the trees, and the quality of the air changed from sappy and oppressive to fresh and biting. Ketaq stopped and turned the mule around. He unloaded my gear, setting it pointedly at my feet. We looked into each other's eyes, and he pointed and nodded slowly, just once. I thanked him, clapping him on the shoulder as is their custom in these parts, and he and the animal set off again through the trees, into the gloom, at a lively pace.

It was too cold to stand and watch him for long. I gathered myself together and shouldered my supplies, suppressing the thought that I had been left here alone, abandoned, and walked in the direction Ketaq had pointed. When I reached the edge of the forest, I stopped and looked out across the glare of fresh white snow. At a distance of quarter, maybe half a mile, it was hard to gauge the distance amidst all the blank, white terrain, like a mirage loomed the monastery. It sat above two terraces with wide steps mounting to a tall central doorway. Contrary to my expectations of an impregnable gate and a gong to strike for admittance, figures could be seen gathered along the breadth of the terraces, climbing the steps, and entering the monastery.

I strode purposefully across the open plateau, watching my boots sink into the snow, glancing up every few paces to check my heading. The closer I came to the shrine, the fewer people were to be seen outside, as if they were all being called back in to some function, such as a meal or meditation. When I reached the steps up to the first terrace, I was quite alone in the stillness and silence of the mountain. I looked about me, at the vista across the dark forest and down to the valley, where the town nestled somewhere out of sight, and up at the gold and black walls and steep roof of the building. The door was now closed, and the terraces were silent. I climbed to the second terrace and approached the door solemnly and respectfully. There was no gong, no handles, and no embroidered bell pull descending from the high eaves; I looked about me once more at the terraces that I had seen thronging with people, at the drifts of snow, and the single set of tracks leading up the steps to my own feet.

What We Believe

Fenja Hill

She didn't believe them. How dare they turn up on her doorstep and frighten her like that? Of course, Michael wasn't dead; he was in Wales, so he couldn't have been on a train to Coventry. They should have checked their facts; she would make a formal complaint. And they had the audacity to ask her to go and look at some poor dead soul and confirm that it was Michael. That was when she had firmly ushered them out of the door, telling them in no uncertain terms that their superiors would be hearing about this. They had told her that her husband was dead, and then, in almost the next breath, made it clear that they didn't even know it was him. The whole thing was outrageous.

Marian went into the kitchen and made herself a cup of tea. She was shaking, and wondered whether something stronger might be a good idea, but they didn't keep much alcohol in the house and anyway, it wasn't even lunchtime. She settled herself in Michael's chair, her guilty pleasure whenever he was away, and sipped at her tea.

Michael had been away a lot since starting the new job, almost a year ago. He was doing so well, and was being groomed for a big promotion. It meant going on courses and visiting other sites, often being away for two or three days at a time. In fact, the very first time had been the induction period for the new job, and that *had* been in Coventry. She even remembered the name of the hotel; The Crown.

This week was the big one though. A five-day leadership skills and team-building combination, somewhere in the Brecon Beacons. There were twenty of them going, from several sites around the country, and anyone who did well was guaranteed almost immediate promotion. It was very intense. Once they arrived, there would be no contact with the outside world, they could not use phones, and they would have to rely on one another for everything. Michael had made it sound very exciting, but Marian thought it was scary. Still, she had encouraged him of course, and had sent him on his way at six this morning with a smile and a kiss. The Newport train left at 7:10 and he had texted to say he was safely on it and that he was turning his phone off now, in preparation for the week ahead.

That was how she knew he hadn't died in a train crash on the way to Coventry. Now that she was calmer, she realised that she could have told the police officers to call his office. Someone there would confirm that he had arrived in Wales, and everything would be fine. But that wasn't her responsibility, it was theirs if they were doing their jobs properly. Who did you complain to about police incompetence? Her knowledge of such things was vague, she would have to look it up.

On Wednesday, a different police officer turned up. This time, she didn't even allow him into the house, but made him stand in the rain as he explained that they were satisfied that the man on the train was her husband and he would like to speak to her....

She closed the door in his face, taking care not to slam it, because she did not want to seem bad-mannered. But really, this was going too far. What was wrong with them? A more gullible woman might have believed all this rubbish and been distraught.

On Friday, Marian went shopping. Michael liked to come back to a home-cooked meal after his days away, eating hotel food, or sandwich platters provided during the office sessions. He was due home at 7:30. The shepherd's pie was on the table at 7:35 and the fresh fruit salad was in the fridge. She hadn't been able to decide between crème fraiche and ice-cream, so there was both.

At 7:45 Marian began to eat. She chatted happily to the empty seat opposite her, not really waiting for responses to her questions, or noticing that the conversation was entirely one-sided. Seeing that Michael had hardly touched his plate, she said she thought it would be best if he went straight to bed; he was clearly worn out by the week's adventures. She bustled about, clearing up and washing the dishes, and then she curled up on the sofa, so that Michael wouldn't be disturbed.

In the morning, Marian decided to leave Michael to sleep in. There was something she needed to do, although she wasn't sure why.

It wasn't possible to get a train to Coventry, because there had been an accident a few days ago and the line was still closed, so Marian traveled by coach and was surprised at how comfortable it was, and how much cheaper than the train. She dozed as the coach sped along the M1, only waking as it pulled into the coach station. With no idea of how to reach the hotel, she decided to take a taxi; a luxury really, but one she could justify because of the cheap coach fare.

Arriving at The Crown, she realised that she had no luggage with her; why was she here? What were her plans? Perhaps she just wanted to see something that had, even briefly, been a part of Michael's life? She didn't think that was it though. Well, she was here now, she would check in for just one night and make some decisions tomorrow. They might not even have a room. Then what would she do?

They did have a room, a small one looking out over a rather lovely park. Was she imagining things, or did the nice young man who checked her in glance up at her when she said her name, with an odd look on his face? Of course he didn't. Or, if he did, it was probably because he wasn't sure how to spell Armitage. Young people these days couldn't spell anything.

Once she had worked out how to use the electronic key, and realised that she had nothing to unpack or to indicate her presence, she went out. She bought a nightdress, a toothbrush and some new underwear. That should be all she would need for one night.

Back in her room, she lay on the bed, wondering what she was expecting to happen. She had come to Coventry because Michael had come here all those months ago. But he wasn't here now, he was home in bed. She realised that she hadn't left him a note to say where she'd gone. He would be worried when he woke up. She tried calling him but he hadn't turned his phone on yet, so she left a message, saying she was doing something important (although she wasn't sure what that was) and would be home tomorrow.

At 7:30, Marian went downstairs to the restaurant. As she was here, she might as well treat this as an adventure and take advantage of all the facilities. She rarely ate out on her own, but she would be fine. And she was hungry; she hadn't eaten since yesterday evening.

Did the pretty young woman in the smart uniform who came to take her order look at her strangely? Did she see faces peering through the steam-smeared glass in the kitchen doorway, to catch a glimpse of her? She had to be imagining things. It was probably lack of food. She'd be fine when she had eaten. She ordered the risotto, something she loved but rarely cooked herself.

Marian rummaged in her handbag for a tissue, suddenly afraid that she might be about to cry. A small sound made her look up.

If Marian could have looked into a mirror of history, this young woman was what she might have seen. From the long, wavy dark hair to the wide eyes and the lips that seemed ready to smile at any moment. Twenty years ago, Marian would have thought she'd found her twin.

There was only one difference.

As the young woman dropped into the seat opposite, tears streaming down her face, her left hand reached hesitantly for Marian's right. Marion barely noticed this though, her eyes fixed on the belly that was straining to escape the restrictions of the hotel uniform.

Train from Hell

Brian Price

The elderly tank engine clanked and wheezed as it crossed the points and pulled its dilapidated coaches alongside the platform. A crisp November wind ruffled the hair and fluttered the skirts of the women lined up to greet the train, but even a gale wouldn't have deterred them from waiting there.

The engine let out a sibilant shriek as it let off steam, and the carriages jerked as the driver braked to a halt. A second's silence was followed by the banging of opening doors slapping against the sides of the coaches, a sound uncomfortably like rifle fire for some of those on board.

Gradually, the train disgorged its passengers. Young men, many still in uniform, some wounded, others apparently unscathed but exhausted, poured onto the platform, their faces haunted by unimaginable sights. With flickering eyes, they searched the assembled throng, almost as if they were scanning for snipers, until they lit upon their mothers, wives or sweethearts. The joy of recognition obliterated, at least temporarily, the marks left by their experiences, and the platform became a melee of embracing couples. Some of them, that could, lifted their partners up and twirled them around. Others simply hugged and kissed, all thoughts of propriety abandoned, and mothers wept as their sons' arms enfolded them. Several of the soldiers met their infant children for the first time and more than a few wondered whether their incomplete and ravaged bodies would still be welcome.

The shouts and laughter died down as the platform emptied, its occupants making haste to return to their homes, families and beds as appropriate. But one woman stood alone and forlorn, uncollected and desperately looking for her fiancé.

Where is he? Oh, God, where is he? They said he would be on this train, she screamed silently. Searching the train, to no avail, she ran to the ticket office, and found a bewhiskered elderly clerk engrossed in the Daily Mirror.

'Help me, please. My fiancé, Billy Robbins, was supposed to be on that train. The army said so. I've looked in all the compartments and he's not there. What's happened to him?'

The clerk lowered his paper and shrugged.

'That's the army for you. Bleedin' inefficient. You'd think they'd know where folks are now the fighting's stopped. Can't help you, I'm afraid, Miss. Maybe he never caught the train. P'raps he'll be on tomorrow's train. Maybe he's still in France. I've got no way of checking. Sorry.'

Raging inside at the man's indifference, she walked disconsolately towards the exit. Then she heard a voice that made her heart leap.

'Hetty! Hetty! It's me!'

She turned around to see Billy walking nonchalantly down the platform a kitbag over his shoulder and his smiling face covered in smuts and coal dust.

'What happened? I thought you were dead in a trench or something. I was terrified.'

'Oh, you know what I'm like with trains. I gave the driver a shilling to let me ride on the footplate. Great fun and much warmer than a third-class carriage. Got a bit mucky though. I reckon I could get a job driving one of them when I'm demobbed.'

Anger, relief and adoration fought for supremacy, the last one winning out.

'You're a swine, Billy Robbins, for scaring me like that.' She threw herself into his arms, sending the kit bag flying. 'But come here my lovely swine and never leave me again.'

As the couple walked off, arm in arm, the curmudgeonly clerk smiled, much to his surprise, then turned his attention back to the racing pages of his paper.

Homeward Bound

Lois Elsden

If I hunched my shoulders I could bring the upturned collar almost to the top of my ears but because the top button was done up I couldn't get my chin inside my coat. Why did I have this stupid prejudice against hats? My attempt at making a bun of hair on top of my head was unsurprisingly unsuccessful, and if I hadn't left my scarf on the train from Manchester, I wouldn't have frost-bitten ears.
It was so bloody freezing, and the wind funnelled along the platform, it was bloody arctic. I'd pulled my hands, bunched into fists, up my sleeves; they would have been deep in my coat pockets except there weren't actual pockets, there was only the appearance of pockets, i.e. just flaps. I suppose it was for style. As for my feet, well, I guess they were still attached to me, I couldn't actually feel them.
 The station master was clumping down the platform, he had big boots on and his thick, navy coat was buttoned to the neck, his cap at a jaunty angle despite the wind.
 "Are you alright, duck, I'm off now, me shift's done and I'm away."
 He'd already told me he'd had to lock everything, and had very kindly let me visit the ladies before that too was locked for the night. He'd had to lock the waiting rooms too, they didn't want any night visitors, he told me.
 I assured him I was fine, pretending to be more cheerful, less miserable than I was. Stiff upper lip - mine was frozen.
 He went out through the entrance and I heard him speaking to someone, several someones by the sound of it. There was a bit of an argument going on, the station master was definitely shirty, it wasn't his fault, he'd been here all day and he was away.
 Two people came onto the platform, the argument continuing between them although I couldn't catch what they were saying. They were two men, one tall and slim, one small and slight. I just hoped they wouldn't sit on a bench near me, I'm sure they were harmless, but being on my own…
 I didn't look their way, I didn't want to encourage conversation. If they'd come into the railway carriage I was in, or if they'd been in the refreshment car and sat near me, I'd have been fine chatting. I've met very interesting people on my various train

journeys, there was the fascinating man with the birthmark splashed across his face as if someone had thrown a glass of wine... We'd had an unexpected conversation about the Etruscans, although I don't remember why. And there had been the other time when a train had broken down and I was fortunately on it in the warm, not waiting for its replacement on a freezing platform as I was now. I'd been sitting next to an interesting elderly lady - straight out of Agatha Christie, and opposite was a young guy from the Welsh National Opera Company - it would have been a great set-up for a crime novel - even better for a film, the opera singer could have sung!

One of the arguing men, the shorter one, walked past me and tried the door of the toilets, which of course was locked. He cursed rather loudly, rather angrily. He was American and it was the damned Brits' fault that he couldn't have a slash.

"Well, fuck it!" he exclaimed and walked to the end of the platform and although he stood round the corner I knew what he was doing.

He came back and rattled the locked door again and walked past me without a glance. His friend was sitting on a bench and had one of his bags on his knee. I didn't stare, I didn't want to do anything to encourage a conversation. When we got on the train, if we ever did get on a train, that would be different.

If only I could nod off to sleep, or if only I was not on my own and could get up and wander about, I was inhibited by my fellow travellers.

The short one walked past me again, and this time he did glance at me, but showed no interest, thank goodness. He tried the door to the waiting room; I'd seen the station master lock it, so no luck for him there. He rattled the handle angrily and began to see if the windows were open - oh, please don't let him break a window to get in! He didn't need to; one hadn't been properly latched and he had it open in a trice and leant inside.

"Hey, hey Tom, I'm in here!"

"Nice, man!" called the other and he stood up, slung his bag over his shoulder and I realised that he had a guitar case with him. He came hurrying past me and fed his bag and guitar through the window to his friend who was now inside. He went back for the other bag and another guitar and passed them into the waiting room.

"Hey miss, do you want a hand climbing in?"

No, no I didn't, but I was so cold now, so very cold now.

"Thank you," and I stood up, really really stiff. My hands were numb and I couldn't hold my case.

The tall man, Tom, picked it up and passed it in to his friend, then helped me clamber out of the cold. With my long coat, frozen feet and numb hands it wasn't the most elegant escape from the biting chill. Inside, although it wasn't warm, there was no wind, thank goodness, no wind.

"Sit by the stove, miss, it's not burning but it's still warm," the short man ordered me. They were younger than I had thought, older than me but only by a couple of years.

I thanked them and subsided onto the bench by the stove, and yes, there was a ghost of heat, and I held my hands to it.

They'd parked themselves at the other end, and were continuing what an on-going squabble about something.

"Say, miss, did the station agent tell you when the next train is due?" one of them called.

"It's the milk train at 4:23," I replied, and I thought, please don't let us have a conversation.

He thanked me and turned back to continue to bicker with his friend and I shut my eyes. They got their guitars out and began to play some folky thing, not my sort of music, but it sent me drifting off into chilly sleep.

The train actually did arrive at 4:23. I'd been woken at four and helped through the window, and we'd stood on the platform and chatted a little. I was heading for Bristol, so would change trains at Birmingham, they were heading to Oxford. I don't know if they'd slept, but we were all tired and slightly grumpy. Then oh, what a welcome sight, coming through the darkness, headlights blazing and with that familiar sound of squeals and puffing, roars and groans, the milk train.

Without a word of farewell, we got into separate carriages, and I fell asleep in the warm, smoky comfort of my onward journey, homeward bound.

Back home, and after I'd caught up with sleep and family and friends, I went shopping and bought new woolly gloves, a warm scarf and a hat.

Something Found in a Book

My Dearest Emilia

Lois Elsden

Isabel gave me several old cookery books when she was clearing her mother's things. I was delighted but it was a while until I actually looked at them. Life hit a busy patch but as September faded away and the evenings were darker, I came across them and began to look through them. 'Madame Prunier's Fish Cookery' written by Ambrose Heath, and with a special introduction by Madame S.B. Prunier herself, 'The Way to a Good Table' by Elizabeth Craig, 'The Happy Housewife' by Ruth Drew, and several others, pre-war and 1950's. I'd probably never use the recipes in them, but they were entertaining and interesting enough to look at.

Somehow I missed Mrs A. B. Marshall's Cookery Book which I came across again a few weeks later. It was beneath a pile of Ngaio Marsh books which I'd bought at the village coffee morning which Isabel and I had wandered into while she was staying.

I settled down with Mrs A.B. Marshall, Agnes Bertha - was she called Aggie by her friends? - and leafed through the old volume. It didn't give its date but referred to her latest publication, 'Fancy Ices' which was published in 1894. In the front was rather a lovely image of Agnes Marshall, confident, striking, interesting. I settled back in my chair, glass of wine at my elbow. I would enjoy looking at this book, and at some point, I would find out more about Agnes.

I turned from the title page to some reviews; *'Cooking has become more than ever a fine art'*, was one, then a special note about the index, and then to the preface. My eye was drawn, however, to the page facing it; in large, flowing script in faded green ink, was a dedication, *'To my dearest Emilia, from your friend "Ever-True", Johnson'*.

Well, how intriguing! Who was Johnson? Who was Emilia? I dabble in genealogy, but there was nothing here which could ever lead me to *Dearest* and *Ever-True*!

Somehow my wine had evaporated, so I went in search of a refill, *'a little wine for thy stomach's sake'* said St Paul. I actually thought it was Dr Johnson, but no, it was St Paul.

Back to Mrs A.B. Marshall and as I picked her up, juggling wine and book, somehow Agnes slipped to the floor. I took a slurp of wine, put it down safely and retrieved Agnes who'd opened, giving me the choice of Thick Lettuce Soup, or Prince Albert Soup. I only glanced at the recipes - Prince Albert involved giblets, and I closed the book and put it back on the shelf beside me.

It was a little later that I noticed a piece of yellow paper on the floor, and picking it up saw it was a brief note, from J to Em. It must have fallen from the book, and it must have been a message from Johnson to Emilia, surely! How intriguing.

I goggled at the brief message - *'E - I beg of you, J'*.

Gosh!

I began to leaf through the recipe book again, difficult as the pages were very thick and had that furry quality that old volumes have.

I found nothing, I would forever wonder about Emilia and Johnson. On the last few pages of the old volume were a series of adverts, many for Agnes's own products, including one for an exquisite and delicately flavoured curry. Opposite was 'highly recommended for culinary and medicinal purposes, Silverrays White Rum.' Across the page in faded purple writing, in galloping cursive script, *'Emilia! How could you forget me! J!'*

Lamb for the Slaughter

Brian Price

It was one of those jobs everyone hates doing. Clearing out a deceased relative's belongings. It fell to me because I had the time, and no-one else was available. So, I put on some shabby clothes, packed a selection of cleaning materials and bin bags into a bucket, and drove to Great Aunt Mildred's Victorian semi on the other side of town.

The house itself was in reasonable condition: structurally sound and without obvious signs of damp, although a mustiness from the unventilated rooms almost overpowered the smell of Cardinal floor polish. The furniture was old-fashioned and sound, but not old enough to be antique and collectable. A charity shop might take it, but a dealer wouldn't be interested. A few pictures on the wall looked pretty, in a kitschy way, but clearly had no great value. There was some nice china though - a few Clarice Cliff pieces and some Susie Cooper. They could go to a specialist and the proceeds would be added to the estate, which was to be divided between my husband and his sister.

Mildred had taken her jewellery with her when she went into the care home, and that was already accounted for. The clothes she had left behind were, sadly, infested with moths and fit only for recycling. In fact, there was very little of a personal nature left and I found it hard to form a picture of a woman I had never met. Perhaps that made my task easier.

After a couple of hours exploring the house, and identifying destinations for the various items present, I decided I needed a coffee break and retrieved my Thermos from my bag. I had found an old biscuit tin at the bottom of a wardrobe and thought I would look through it while my drink cooled. It contained a few personal documents – birth certificates, house deeds, her husband's death certificate – and some letters and Christmas cards, although surprisingly few of the latter. But, at the bottom, was a collection of newspaper cuttings which nearly made me spill my coffee. Aunt Mildred had been tried for murder!

The yellowed collection of newsprint described how Mildred Gathorn, nee Harrison, had been arrested and charged with murdering her husband. During the course of an eight-day trial at Winchester Assizes, she was accused of killing her husband, John, in order to inherit his money and elope with a local pharmacist with whom, it was alleged, she was having an affair. The pharmacist had dispensed John Gathorn's heart medicine, and the prosecution alleged that Mildred had persuaded him to supply much stronger tablets than John required, with fatal results.

As the trial continued, duly sensationalised by the popular press, things were looking grim for the defendant, until the defence case was presented. Mildred's barrister, Raymond Drake, a shy-looking man with a deceptive appearance but rapier-like cross-examination skills, first drew blood by forcing the police inspector running the case to confirm that the pharmacist had been arrested, a week previously, on suspicion of committing gross indecency with a choirboy. This clearly undermined the prosecution's allegation of an affair. He then called an independent analyst, who confirmed that John Gathorn's heart tablets, a form of digitalis, were of the normal strength. Further evidence for the defence came from the examination of the pharmacist's records, which demonstrated that there were no missing heart drugs and that every tablet received had been properly dispensed, in accordance with prescriptions.

Recalling the pathologist to the witness box, Mr Drake elicited the admission that, yes, John Gathorn could have had a heart attack, even with the medication, through natural causes. Asked whether an accidental overdose of the tablets could have caused a lethal reaction, the pathologist admitted that it could, although there was some dispute over the exact deadly dose of that particular drug. The pathologist confirmed that a partly dissolved tablet, of normal strength, had been found in the stomach of the deceased, who had recently dined on roast lamb, mint sauce and roast potatoes.

After the jury deliberated for six and a half hours, the foreman returned a not guilty verdict, and my husband's great aunt was acquitted.

Well, that was a juicy story, I thought, as I rinsed out my cup. My husband had never mentioned it, but perhaps he never knew. I then turned my attention to Mildred's books. There were a few old copies of Dickens and other Victorian writers. No first editions or collectable volumes, as far as I could tell. The charity shop for them, I thought. Then I caught sight of a familiar name. Mrs Beeton. My gran had been given Mrs Beeton's Everyday Cookery by my grandad when they got married in the thirties. This was obviously an earlier edition, and I leafed through it out of curiosity. I came across the page describing a recipe for mint sauce and, as I did so, a slip of paper fell out. Scribbled across it, in fine pencilled writing, were the words *finely chop an ounce of foxglove leaves and add to the sauce, with extra sugar and mint to disguise the taste. Don't eat more than a quarter-teaspoonful of the sauce.*

I could hardly believe what I was reading. So, my husband's distant relative was a murderer after all, probably aided and abetted by the pharmacist, who would have known about the toxic properties of foxgloves. But how had they got away with it? Wouldn't the pathologist have ordered an analysis of the stomach contents as well as the partly-dissolved tablet?

Something jogged my memory, and I returned to the collection of newspaper cuttings. One of them had seemed out of place. The headline was brief - *Doctor's assistant dismissed for misconduct.* The short article which followed described how Albert Harrison, an assistant at the hospital mortuary, had been sacked for an alleged incident of drunkenness, which had led to the accidental destruction of post-mortem samples, needed for several important trials, before they could be analysed. One of these trials was great aunt Mildred's and, when I saw the miscreant's name, I realised exactly what had happened. For Albert Harrison was Mildred's brother and, by bribery or coercion, he had been persuaded to destroy John Gathorn's stomach contents.

I was flabbergasted by the cunning that my husband's great aunt and her fellow conspirators had shown. I hadn't realised what lay beneath the veneer of respectability that covered my husband's distant family. And, much as I trust my husband, I had a feeling I wouldn't want to eat mint sauce for a while – and certainly not any made to Great Aunt Mildred's special recipe.

Fields of Attraction

Macaque

Magnetism is a strange force. I remember copying the patterns made by iron filings revealing the magnetic fields of those red and silver bar magnets at school. I remember trying to push like poles together, feeling their spongy reluctance; and that unstoppable attraction of opposite poles, that sensation in my careful fingers when the force would overcome my attempts to find and balance on its edge. I used to love science, the experiments, the apparatus. I used to love the winter terms, when we would have Bunsens burning on the desks for warmth; how we could change the flame with the little collar, and forge works of art from our plastic geometry sets. We would distil crude oil into butane, petroleum and sludge; test acids and alkalis with Litmus; wrap match heads in tin foil and make rockets; study skin and saliva samples under microscopes; turn out the lights and float sodium on blotting paper until the water soaked through and caused a frenzy of bright spitting sparks. For some reason, though, I liked magnetism best; one of the invisible forces of attraction, like gravity, and love.

I didn't grow up to be a scientist, although my friends and colleagues have often dubbed me The Mad Professor over the years thanks to my untameable hair and a certain propensity for stream of consciousness mutterings. Sometimes I do it deliberately to see what I can get away with; It's quite amazing how much leeway people give you if they think you are foreign or on a spectrum. All the same, I should have liked to really study such forces, like Newton with his apple. What does draw people to certain things, to certain other people? Where do the connections end? Can we apply these forces of attraction to ghosts and hauntings? Could I have made a career out of these enquiries instead of heading a marketing department and wishing I could open a bookshop?

I happen to be drawn to books; magnetically, hypnotically, indefatigably and unfailingly. Like an apple to the ground or a north to a south pole. Books are irresistible to me. Cut out words and sprinkle them over me like iron filings and you would see the fields of attraction radiating in search of books. And so it was that I came to be rummaging excitedly through boxes of donated tomes at the village hall's charity sale. I have never had the sort of luck that one reads about sometimes: people picking up a pamphlet for 50p in a bric-a-brac bin only to discover it's an original *Unicorn* by Angela Carter or a copy of *The Waste Land* written in Eliot's own hand, but every box of miscellaneous volumes holds limitless promise. I had already picked out a well-thumbed Derek Tangye, and a very clean copy of an Ian M Banks that I didn't have, when, amongst the cookbooks, crime thrillers and dog-eared Mills & Boons, I came across something familiar. It was the same cat notebook that my grandma had once given me, which I had filled with my adolescent poetry. I had treasured it, and at some point, in my damp university digs, it had become water damaged, the spine softening and flaking, mildew staining the pages and smudging the ink; I had been heartbroken. I recognised the twee cover immediately: the hand-drawn words 'The Cat Notebook Being An Illustrated Book With Quotes' surrounded a yellow cat with blue eyes caressing with one paw what looked to be a nettle. I opened it near the middle and flicked through the pages, delighting once again in the pencil sketches and quotations, remembering on certain pages which poems I had tried so hard to scribe neatly. Inside the front cover I noticed it had been published in 1985; that would have been about right. I happily paid £2.50 for my three gems, and sauntered home with a joyful spring in my step.

I popped the two books on the sideboard, and sat at my desk with the notebook, reminiscing about my grandma. When I was younger, she had been on a coach trip to Warwick Castle and bought me another notebook and pen set from the gift shop, tightly sealed in plastic. "I thought you would like this," she had said, handing it to me, the etched image of the castle prominent on the cover; then as I opened it, she had asked with genuine interest, "What is it?". The memory made me smile; I felt sure I still had that little book tucked away in the attic, once again filled with poetic scribblings, but for now my attention was drawn to the cat book. It was like I was in a time warp, holding this pristine copy thirty-five years later. I opened the book reverently. There was a page before the title page, with a black cat poised about to leap from a branch, and I remembered that I had written a poem inspired by Norman MacCaig's *Frogs* here, which began 'Cats purr more frenzied than anything purrs.' Then came the title page, with a mother cat and kitten touching noses. The fur, ears, whiskers, and the lively eyes in the drawings were superb, truly feline. I turned to the first page and discovered that the notebook was not, in fact, blank. How had I failed to spot an entry on the first page? In copperplate curls, someone had written 'I bought this book in Richmond because I couldn't resist it. I have just spent a wonderful three days with my parents. We really enjoyed ourselves.' The facing page was blank, but when I turned it over, there were details of random events with dates: an OU application form arriving, a barbeque with some colleagues (at which Johnathan had been very mature), seminars attended (one was 'brilliant'), all during June and July 1989. On the following page, a year later, somebody called Peter had been transferred to Newcastle 'for three months – but who knows? Total devastation!'

Who had thrown this book out? Who had found it so irresistible that weekend in Richmond, then barely used it? Surely no-one would knowingly donate something so personal to a charity book stall; sparse as it was, it still resembled a diary. I was gleaning insights into this stranger's life. I wanted to know more about Peter; how long had he actually spent in Newcastle? Did they keep in touch? I wanted to know about the Open University, and about Johnathan; was he a child, or did he have issues, that his maturity could be so remarkable?

Some blank pages followed, and I thought this little window into somebody else's past had closed. I was about to turn back and look over the entries again – it seemed to me such an odd way to use a book that I had been quite meticulous about, gauging which poems would fit on each page in the space left by the illustrations – but then there was a longer entry on a page marked by a quote from a twelve-year-old girl about a cat being loved by everyone but loving only himself. Another nine months had passed since the entry about Peter, the date at the top of the entry being 13/4/91. The words were laid out like a poem, the sentences truncated and not filling the width of the page. Squeezed at a slant between the date and the entry, the words 'Brian's mum died' had clearly been added afterwards. I read and reread the entry:

> 'The funeral was lovely
> Sad, but full of
> Warm memories
> The Church was full
> Sarah played the organ
> Jane and Simon clung to each other
> Johnathan was incredibly grown up and self-contained
> Brian withdrew into himself
> Jane wanted him, Simon wanted Jane
> Johnathan wanted no one

No one wanted me
I wished I was somewhere else
It is the way things are
That is all.'

My throat tightened and my chest contracted. Such unexpected raw emotion. So many fields of attraction crossing and converging in so few lines. I went over those names again and again:

'Jane wanted Brian, Simon wanted Jane
Johnathan wanted no one
No one wanted me'

How had I come to possess these words? Had anybody else read them, I wondered? Where had the notebook come from? One of my neighbours? The author's children, perhaps? Thirty-odd years is a long time. But for the book to have been kept so long, unused after the funeral, and now discarded to be picked up by a stranger: I was overwhelmed by the sense of tragedy it exuded. Who were these people so intricately linked? What had happened to them? I noticed there was no mention of Peter in the last entry; no mention of who the author might have been drawn to. So much intrigue, and so much left untold. The rhythm of those three lines haunted me. The pain, the resignation, the finality; 'That is all.' What could I possibly use this book for, now? Could anything I wrote ever match these words for their honesty and emotion?

'No one wanted me.' Was that true, I wondered? Was the previous owner of this quaint little book pole-less, unmagnetized? What are the lode stones in life that give us our charges, that align us to our desires and our fates? Is this science or philosophy I'm considering, now? And if we had the knowledge, what then? It's not as if scientific achievement has ever come without a cost.

I pressed the book closed and held it tightly, almost ceremonially. I had certainly got far more than I had bargained for with my fifty pence. I slipped the notebook into the middle drawer of the desk and went to make a cup of tea. I was glad I had found the book; I felt privileged to have read those few unexplained pages. I would come back to it. I took my tea through to the sitting room and picked up the Banks; Derek Tangye had had a cat, I recalled.

Something Overheard

Café au Hate

Brian Price

He had that sort of voice which showed he'd developed complaining almost to the status of a martial art. Not only was he proud of this skill, he wanted everyone else to appreciate it, which is why his voice resounded round the bookshop café, disturbing those who were working on theses, writing novels or simply looking at the paper over a coffee.

It started with a moan about the buses. How he had to walk a couple of hundred yards from the stop to the shop, as if the city transport system should have been organised purely around his needs. Then it was immigrants, speaking funny, taking jobs and houses. The facts that much of the city's infrastructure depended on people whose origins were outside the UK, and the brown-skinned bus driver had a city accent as broad as his own, were lost on him.

He really got into his stride when he turned his sights on the NHS.

"I had to wait forty minutes for an assessment in the eye clinic and they had all these people watching me. In training, they said they were. I don't know what the NHS is coming to," he grumbled, oblivious to the point that the party he had clearly voted for was responsible for the underfunding of the service, and also that his assessment was not the most urgent of cases on the list.

Next, it was the turn of the café staff. The young woman serving, on her own, was clearly doing her best to cope with a sudden influx of customers, all ordering complex drinks or food that had to be cooked. A wait was inevitable, and most customers accepted this with good grace. Not this one. He complained to the server and also to the colleague who came to join her shortly after. Then he complained about the cake he bought – "a bit stale, isn't it?" - despite the fact that he had seen it being removed from the chiller less than half an hour previously. He also didn't like the fact that the coffee supplier had changed and his latte didn't taste quite the way it did the previous week.

By now, his constant moaning had attracted the attention of other customers. Some of them looked on him with disgust and others simply laughed at him. A few changed seats to avoid overhearing his tirade. But the person I felt most sorry for was his wife who sat in front of him, drooping like the Liz Truss lettuce.

'Does she get this all the time?' I wondered. 'Does he use her as a verbal punchbag at home? I'll bet he finds fault with her cooking, her cleaning, her appearance and just about everything else.' I watched her for a while, discreetly. She never spoke, but occasionally nodded her head in automatic agreement with his words. Once, I saw a flash of steel in her eyes, but it passed, almost instantly.

As I finished my coffee and got up to leave, there was a commotion from the complainer's table. He had fallen forward in his seat, knocking crockery and cutlery onto the floor and creating a hell of a mess. No doubt he'll complain about the stain on his trousers, I thought. But then I realised it was serious.

"Help! My husband!" shouted the woman. "He's had a heart attack!"

Staff rushed to the table and tried CPR, while someone else went in search of the defibrillator, located elsewhere in the shopping mall. It was too late. 'Perhaps he's complained himself to death,' I thought, uncharitably. But then I thought of his crushed and downtrodden widow. The widow who was now standing up straight, a brightness in her eyes which had hitherto been absent, accepting the condolences of those around her with quiet dignity. 'She'll be better off without that 24/7 misery-guts,' I reckoned.

As I walked out of the shop into the rainy streets, I had a short flashback. When the moaner turned round to glare at a student whose laptop had emitted a short bleep on starting up, did I see the woman drop something into his coffee? Surely not. But on the other hand...

I opened my umbrella, headed for home and mused on the concept of karma.

(Inspired by a conversation overheard in Waterstones in The Galleries, Bristol)

Day Tripper

Macaque

    The boat to Caldey Island plunged gamely on the swell, spray cool in the hot sun, and over the engine the coarse caw of gulls. No, my ear relented, not gulls this time, but a family from Manchester, down for a week's holiday with their loud voices and harsh vowels. The mother was a short, stout woman with Italian features and close-cropped black hair, the father looked like the Milky Bar Kid gone to seed. The two chubby children were squabbling, it seemed, but it was only the parent's voices that rose above the noise of the boat: "Stop mytherin', Tara," and "Don't do that, ye'll break it." I turned my attention back to the island and the prow of the vessel cutting its way through the undulating blue between us. At least they weren't Brummies.
    My earliest memory of a car journey is the sound of the windscreen wipers. Not the sound the rubber blades sometimes make nowadays, this was an old car made in the 60's, and the motor that operated the wipers made a hypnotic two-tone continuo, a glissando with a Doppler effect, a bit like a bored donkey. The Brummy accent always reminds me of those wipers and the seemingly interminable motorway journey.
    Disembarking at Caldey's stone wharf, I headed quickly for the path that led up the cliff, freeing my camera from my rucksack as I hurried along, but I could still hear them behind me: "Walk normal, Paul, ye've only been at sea twenty minutes!" I thought I might actually find them quite amusing to listen to, but they were just too loud for this monastic setting. The lighthouse, abbey and chocolate factory were all signposted by sky blue arrows with cloud-white writing, but there was really only one path on the whole island. A noticeboard announced two scheduled tours of the abbey, the last one at three o'clock, and stated that as it was home to a strict order of monks, no women were allowed to enter. I thought I would start with the lighthouse, hoping that the family would be heading for the chocolate factory, and join the last tour having explored the rest of the island.
    The conditions were perfect. The august heat was tempered by the gentle sea breeze, the sky was a deep blue but not empty, with just enough cumulus clouds to provide photographic balance. I passed the abbey and the post office and the little green dotted with

benches, and was soon walking a grassy track beside a dry-stone wall. Once past the chocolate factory that was housed in the buildings of an old farm, the wall ended, and the pale trodden path led on through waving grass towards the lighthouse, like moonlight over a bay.

    I spent a few pleasant hours photographing the lighthouse, the rocks, the old watch tower, and all the other scenes of aesthetic interest. I visited the chocolate factory, of course, and browsed the perfume shop and other industrious outlets that the monks used to support themselves. I found the tea room and sat outside to enjoy a rustic ploughman's and a refreshing ale, and was not surprised by the return of the Mancunians. We were a small boat party on a small island, after all. They were sitting on one of the benches on the nearby green, picnicking on food from the mother's voluminous shoulder bag. Afterwards, the father produced a block of Caldey Island chocolate, and broke a row of squares off for the little girl. He was less successful with the next row, breaking just a corner off with his thumb, as the sarcastic older boy called out "Oh, god, be careful, you'll give me diabetes with a piece that size!"

    "Don't be cheeky, or ye'll get nowt," replied his dad.

    I smiled to myself, and sipped my beer, checking the time for the tour round the abbey. Similar thoughts must have been occurring on the green, for there was an almighty outburst of "That's not fair, it's so not fair! How come he gets to go round the abbey but I can't? Why can't girls go in? Oo do these monks think they are?" peppered with "Tara, calm down. Tara, stop showing me up, will ye!" It was definitely time to make my way to the abbey.

    In all fairness, she didn't really miss much. I think the boy and his father only really appreciated the half hour or so of peace and quiet. When the tour had finished, I began to head back towards the jetty, but was distracted once again by the harsh tones of the girl's raised voice.

    "Anyway, Paul, *I'm* going into the ladies', and *you* can't go in *there!*" I could almost hear the sticking out of a tongue before she stomped off inside the little whitewashed building.

Something Overheard

Lois Elsden

"Do you mind if we sit here?" one of them asked - well I say asked, she was actually telling me that they were going to sit here.
"No, not all, plenty of room," I lied. I had just bought coffee and an Eccles cake, Tim is renowned for his Eccles cakes, I'm sure most of the people come here just to treat themselves. I do like his Eccles cakes, but I come here because I find it conducive to writing. The murmur of other customers, the hiss and wheeze of the coffee machine, no BGM - background music, enough going on to inspire if I'm running out of words, but not enough to distract - usually.
The women who had just come in, pulling off their hats and closing their umbrellas were excited to be out of the rain and exclaiming loudly exactly how horrid it was, how unseasonable. I had settled myself at the table in the corner, most people like to sit by the windows, or in the little room through the arch. I always thought of this as 'my' table, although I was happy enough to sit anywhere else along the wall. The other, smaller room through the archway always seemed a bit chilly.
The women were settling on the table adjacent to mine and they didn't really need to ask my permission to sit there. I couldn't tell them the truth, that I'd prefer them to sit further away, preferably in a different café because they sounded a convivial and noisy gang and I knew they would be a distraction.
The door flung open again, and the two new women blown in on a gale were greeted as if they'd returned from some far flung clime.
"Celia! How lovely of you to come, you must have set off at the crack of!"
"I was on the fast train, got me here in no time!"
"It's not the distance, Celia, it's how far it is to get here!"
I tried to ignore my noisy neighbours who were now taking it in turns to embrace Celia and her friend, taking their coats and umbrellas as if they owned the place and asking what they wished to drink. It seemed Celia had been on a trip to the Holy Land, I heard her say it was like travelling through the Bible. The loudest of the original women to have arrived, Sarah, announced '*I've done the Nile - twice!*'

They sat down on the next table, some greeted me as if they thought I was part of their gang. I nodded, mumbled, and focused on my screen. *Please don't let them ask what I'm writing,* I implored the gods of story-telling.

I shouldn't have even thought that.

"I say, are you a writer?" Someone had sat down on the chair diagonally opposite me - *on my table!* I mumbled something and stared at what I'd written.

"I love poetry, are you a poet? My current favourite was discussed on Poetry Please, I can't remember his name, but maybe you know him?"

I can't tell you what my answer would have been if I hadn't bitten my tongue pretty thoroughly. I hadn't listened to the programme, I replied.

"David Penhaligon? Was it David Penhaligon, he writes poetry, doesn't he?"

Loud-mouth Sarah must have caught what was said because she announced in a loud, patronising voice that surely Judy knew that David Penhaligon was a Cornish MP, who died donkeys years ago, tragically young in a road accident. Well that ended that conversation.

How could I escape this horror? I closed my laptop; I'd pack up and go, even though I was in full flow and my story was racing in my head.

Just as I decided that, the door flung open again as if the wind had decided to join the party, and two sodden women staggered in and with some difficulty closed the door behind them. There was no way I was going to leave with this tumult happening outside. However, I reckoned there may be spare seats through the arch in the other room. So I stood up, gathered my things, made some amiable and friendly remarks to those of the women who weren't shrieking a welcome to the new arrivals, and sidled into the other room.

"Coffee and Eccles?" Tim called as I passed - *coffee and tea-cake, please,* I called back. His teacakes were massive, no joke intended, and I was now in need of sustenance.

The little room had a few customers sitting quietly, but there was one free table. It was, unfortunately, somewhat near the main room, but at least my ears were no longer ringing. I sat down, my back to a couple of gentlemen in walking gear who were quietly discussing books and films. *Enys Men,* one of them said. I must catch up with that, it was a fascinating Cornish film from the reviews

I'd read. *Salvation Johnny,* said the other - crikey, who was that by? I may have read it many, many years ago, but the author was now lost to me in the mists of time.

Tim brought me my coffee and teacake and he'd given me an extra pat of butter, maybe making up for the carry-on next door. They were harmless, those women, just so pleased to see eachother and loud and thoughtless... No, I revised my opinion, they were obnoxious, extremely annoying and very inconsiderate. At least I wasn't sitting near them but I might as well have been!

"I've got sugar all over my pants!"someone screamed to a cacophony of laughter.

"Just 'cos I like coasters because coasters are something you can use!" I'm sure that was Judy.

"I did like it but I thought, don't get carried away, Jeanette," said Jeanette.

"Why don't you get carried away Jeanette, you deserve it for once!" cried Celia.

"Alison has a wedding dress, Juicy, in darkly pink across the bottom!" I'm sure there was no-one called Juicy there, it must have been Judy, but my head was ringing, even as I wondered if there was such a colour as darkly pink.

"I've not done anything illegally..."

Oh good grief, however vile the weather, I was going to have to escape!

"So what did Marian do exactly with the horsewhip? What did she say to Bobby which was so..."

Suddenly their voices dropped and all I could hear was a faint murmur of women's voices. I never did find out what Marian did - it was something to do with "*vegan trifle? Actual vegan trifle, Sasha's recipe?*"

Later, when they had all departed to their lunch in a nearby pub, as the downpour abated, Tim told me they were the Women Unleashed Luncheon Club.

"But where they came from I don't know! Better than the evangelical lot from Huish Episcopi who come in for coffee on a Tuesday, after a morning of going round the village, saving people from Satan!"

I must remember *not* to come and try and write here on Tuesdays.

(Most of the overheard conversations of the ladies above were actually overheard by me, a real group of

women meeting for coffee - but I will not disclose the location!)

Cloak

In the Coppice Wood

Macaque

Jordy

Cloke's dead.

Art

Next day, Jordy found Mr Cloke, another neighbour, dead in the wood. This just wasn't natural, now.

Leeza

Thorn was still missing the next morning. Arthur was cooking up the bacon when I woke, don't know if he slept all, think he must of stayed up in the armchair with the rifle on his lap all night. He said he'd go find John first thing, and I should get on with my chores as normal, just take Jordy with me, keep a watch over him. The three of us had our breakfast in silence, but there was nothing else we could do. We told Jordy we'd just have to wait for Thorn to come home. Everything would be alright. Don't know quite when we started lyin' to each other and all. I could tell Art was worried now, even if he tried not to show it for Jordy.

Art

I stayed up all night waiting for Thorn. We locked all the doors, so I wanted to be there to open up if he came back in the middle of the night. I dozed, off and on, but he never came. I would have heard him for sure. Something's definitely not right, not since Old Mr Rhope turned up on our stretch of river. I had an uneasy feeling about the whole thing.

Leeza

We went out to the barn to pick up my shoulder bag. Barn was quiet, different quiet to when Thorn's up in the attic sleeping. Eerie quiet. We didn't stay long, I just grabbed my things, and we set off. I thought we'd go down towards the river, have another look for clues in the daylight, but Jordy said he wanted to go up to the woods. Man, that boy's like some sort of blood hound, you know. It ain't natural the way he is, and him only six. Thorn's right about his magic ways, I reckon.

Jordy

I been dreaming about the woods. Rhope's eye been staring down like the moon, looking through the trees, through the trees one minute then right at me the next. I knew I had to go to them woods.

Leeza

Jordy was real quiet. I guess I thought it had to do with Thorn. I tried to make light of it, tried to get him talking, but in the end we just walked in silence. I was distracted too, of course. Thinking about Thorn, and the gate, and Mr Rhope. I was wondering if we might find the wood piles tampered with or something. One of the stacks had fallen over, but that happens. Especially in a storm, and I hadn't been up here since the storm, what with the gate to mend and then Mr Rhope and all. I started to restack the lengths. I could hear Jordy tramping about in the trees.

Thorn

Sun was up and warming when I got back. I was starting to dry off by the time I reached the house. No signs of anybody about, guess they hadn't missed me much. Arthur had left a note on the kitchen table, and some cooked bacon under a cloth. I was grateful for that. He said he had gone to speak to John. They were all worried about me. This business with Mr Rhope sure has got everybody fair rattled. Was a time I could stay out all night and nobody bothered. Nobody left me bacon and notes.

Leeza

So then it happens again. The rustling stops for a minute, or I get used to it and block it out. Then it turns to a thundering and a crashing, the cracking of twigs like chicken bones, and Jordy comes runnin' out the trees and he says Cloke's dead. That's two of 'em, now. I said I was done with praying and all, but I looked up to the sky, then, wondering.

Jordy

Cloke was lyin' amid the ground cover, all the twigs and leaves and that. The wood is untidy, ain't nobody got time for picking up any little bits. Arthur says it's good for the soil and the bugs and all. Anyway, he lyin' there all still, look like he maybe been up to town, he wearin' this red-brown suit. Then I gets up close, all quiet, like, and he ain't wearin' no suit, he all covered in blood, like he been got by some animal. Not the sky wolf, this time, this was diff'rent.

Leeza

He took me to look at the body. It was gruesome alright. Savaged by somethin' for sure. I don't want to think none more about it. Maybe he tried to find shelter in the trees. Must have been at night, in the pitchness, ain't no use tryin' to hide in a coppice, anyone could see that much in daylight. Not a tree worth climbing or hidin' behind anyhow.

Art

John was in his kitchen when I walked up the lane. He came to the door when he heard my gravel crunch. I forgot all about the court men and the legal papers and all what I was going to tell John yesterday, I just blurted out that Thorn had gone missing and been out all night. He ushered me in and poured me a mug of chicory from the pot on the stove. He told me to sit and tell him what had happened, when I had last seen Thorn, while he finished his own breakfast. Then he said we'd best take another look by the river.

Thorn

I ate up the bacon with my fingers and put on some hot coffee, then I changed out of my damp clothes. From my window, I saw Arthur and John crossing the yard in the direction of the river. I ran down the stairs and followed them, shouting for them to hold up. Art started to rage at me, but John put a hand on his shoulder to calm him. John asked me if I was alright. They wanted to know where I had been, so I told them. That was my intention, anyway, they needn't have asked, really.

Leeza

I left my work bag and tools by the wood stacks and me and Jordy ran back to the house. When we got there, Jon and Thorn were with Arthur in the kitchen, all calm, like, and Art was pouring three mugs of coffee. They looked at us funny when we came bustin' in, and we looked funny back. Nobody was expectin' what everybody saw.

Jordy

Cloke's dead. I had a dream about where to find him. Old Rhope's missin' eye been hauntin' me and showin' me stuff. What we gonna do now, though, the dream didn't say.

Cloak

Lois Elsden

She got on my nerves straight away by disputing my name. "C - L - O - K - E."

"No," I told her firmly and, just about politely, "Cloak, 'C - L - O - A - K.'"

"But that's an item of clothing. As a name, it's Cloke."

"I think I ought to know my own name by now, it was my father's family name, and unusually, my mother was also - very distantly, a Cloak, as in the item of clothing."

"Well, your badge says Cloke," she insisted.

"In that case, it's not mine, and nor is the lanyard you're obviously trying to give me."

I left her in the vestibule and strolled through to the theatre bar, following the chalked arrow on the blackboard resting on an easel.

I had thought about joining the Unique and Unusual Name Society for a while. I'd stalked their social media pages, and looked at their webpage - the frontispiece only as I wasn't a member. I should have got a drift of them from the fact that it actually said *'as a non-member you only have access to our frontispiece.'*

Cloak was on their list, I knew that much, along with Cloake, Cloke, Clokey, and Clokie - oh and Kloke with a K. How many of these homophonous Cloaks would be present I didn't know, maybe none, but there was only one I was interested in.

Would they even be here? The Cloak I was interested in was on their membership, which, in this area, even across several counties, was small. I'd travelled here to Easthope especially for their event but I was beginning to think I was going about this in a crazy and ridiculous way.

I pushed open the fancy double doors which would lead into the auditorium, the U.U.N.S. Convocation - *what pretension* - was gathering on the stage of the small theatre for drinks and canapés before retiring to the green room for dinner.

I wandered down the aisle and round to the steps leading up to the stage. Someone else was standing at the bottom with a clipboard, and smiled welcomingly as I approached. This was an improvement.

"You don't seem to have a lanyard," she said pleasantly. I agreed that I hadn't got a lanyard and told her my name was Isabel Cloak, Isabel with an 'a' and one 'l', Cloak with an 'oa'. She apologised, clearly distressed that I wasn't on the list. "I seem to have got in a muddle, because I have a lanyard here for an Isobelle - with an 'o', a double 'l' and an 'a', but she is Cloke -"

I interrupted. "Cloke as in C-l-o-k-e?"

She nodded, confused.

"Can you point Isabel Cloke out to me, please," I asked nicely, because she was being nice.

She pointed to a blond woman with a rather large chest, holding forth to a gaggle of folk with unique and unusual names.

I mounted the wooden steps to the stage and without a pause, or a second, or even first thought, strode across to her.

"Good evening," I said in an attention-seeking voice. "You seem to have got my lanyard, are you also under the impression that you are me. I am Isabel Cloak, and I believe you are in fact Isobella Cloke!"

I wish I'd been able to glance around, because no doubt the faces around me reflected many and various expressions.

I wish I had been able to say *'Give me my lanyard, imposter, and be gone!'* However, I restrained myself and began the usual old rigmarole of *"You do not have to say anything. But it may harm your defence if you do not mention when questioned..."* as the constable who had trailed in behind me, handcuffs at the alert, clumped up and took her arm.

There was a terrific kerfuffle as you might imagine, and I was sorry, because really I would have liked to stay and find out more about U.U.N.S. but impersonating a police officer is a serious matter, especially when the officer is me.

Lost Property

Brian Price

"Gentleman's left his cloak behind," announced the cloakroom attendant to the front-of-house manager. "Looks expensive, too."

"Didn't you see him go out, Millie? Couldn't you have stopped him?"

"Funnily enough, Mr Fenton. I didn't. So I couldn't."

"Well, what did he look like?"

"I can't really remember much about him. He was tall, I think. Smartly dressed. Normally I'm good with faces but he just didn't register, y'know?"

"There's no-one like that still in the auditorium. Just some girl who's fallen asleep in the stalls. Clearly Pinter was lost on her."

"Perhaps she's still waiting for Godot," Millie giggled.

"Very funny. I'd better go and wake her. The Alhambra is a theatre, not a doss house. I don't suppose there's a name in the cloak, is there?"

"No Mr Fenton. No label at all."

"Put it in the lost property cupboard then, with a note of today's date. I expect the owner will collect it. Probably overindulged in the bar during the interval and forgot about it."

While Millie complied, Fenton walked wearily through the doors that led to the stalls. He longed to get home and take the weight off his feet, and patrons who overstayed their welcome were a nuisance.

"Come along, please, miss," he called. "Time to go home."

There was no reply from the young woman, slumped in the back row. He called again, eased himself between the rows of seats and shook her shoulder. Her head fell back and Fenton stood transfixed, unable to breathe. His eyes locked on the two bright red puncture marks on the woman's neck.

"Millie," he yelled. "Come quickly…no…don't. Fetch a priest. Now."

The woman's eyes opened slowly. A lascivious smile spread across her face as Fenton stared, unable to move. Her lips parted, revealing two unusually long teeth. She lunged at the hypnotised theatre manager. And at the top of the theatre a bat, energised by its recent meal, flew swiftly out of an open skylight and into the night.

The writers

Anne Bunn

Anne has been bothered and bewildered by the need to write stories from her earliest years as a proud Channel Islander, but despite keeping a notebook by her bed for midnight inspiration, life kept intervening!

The poetry bug hit much later, but now the two vie for her undivided attention, and nothing and no one is safe from her attempts to encapsulate her responses in words.

Being drawn back into the writing fold by engaging first with Chapter One creative writing group, she then tried her hand at local Poetry Slams, is a member of Weston Poets, and delighted to be welcomed as a newbie to Writers in Stone.

Lois Elsden

Lois Elsden is passionate about writing; she was born and brought up in Cambridge, and having spent most of her adult life in Manchester, she now lives in a small Somerset village by the sea.

Lois writes full time and has published twenty books, including two anthologies with other writers. She has written eight mystery novels, a guide to creative writing *So You Want to Write*, and three novels for reluctant readers.

Her Radwinter series of seven genealogical mysteries follows Thomas Radwinter's commissions to explore family history. However, he finds himself unexpectedly embroiled in other cases, including kidnapping, abduction, attempted murder, secret sects and haunted hotels... oh and stalkers and serial killers. The final (perhaps) instalment will be published in 2024.

Lois belongs to two writing collectives, 'Writers in Stone' and 'The Moving Dragon Writes'; she leads creative writing and family history writing groups, travels round the country to live music events, and watches the world go by in her local pub.

You can read Lois's blog on WordPress.

Fenja Hill

Fenja Hill is the self-published author of **Nightwriting**, a multi-genre collection of stories combining humour with a dark edge, and **Happy Endings are Overrated** which combines the dark edge with wonderful insight. Her poem *Traveling in the Back Seat* was shortlisted for the 2022 Yeovil Literary Prize and her short story

Taking Notes took second place at the 2023 Wells Literary Festival. *An Idea of Heaven* was shortlisted for the Burnham Book Festival short story prize 2024

Elizabeth Lawrence

Elizabeth Lawrence's usual flowing pen has been staunched this year, due to health issues. She has, nonetheless, derived great pleasure from writing these short stories, and hopes the readers will enjoy them too.

Macaque

Macaque is a poet and author living in rural Somerset. Publications include *Palimpsest of Ghosts* (2017), **The Strange Discoveries at Wimblestone Road** (2021), *Mosaic* (2022), **The Atrocious Parrot** (2022) and **Dryad** (2024) with a contribution from Joanne Harris. His story *For the Record* won the Burnham Book Festival short story prize 2024.

Simon Phelps

Simon joined at the end of 2022, and has published two historical fiction novels, **No Man's Son** and **Blood on the Water**. He joins the group when not touring the continent in his camper.

Brian Price

Brian Price is a retired scientist and environmentalist who probably reads more crime fiction than is good for him. He is the author of **Crime writing: how to write the science**, a guide for crime writers, and also a number of short stories. His first novel, **Fatal Trade**, was published in 2021 and his second, **Fatal Hate**, was published in 2022 followed by **Fatal Dose** and **Fatal Blow** both published in 2023. His fifth novel, Fatal Image, is due out in late 2024. He has been a member of Writers in Stone since February 2019.

Index of writers

Ann Bunn

Cyberspace	11
Linking Up	13

Lois Elsden

Shadows of the Cinnamon Apple Trees	22
Crime View	32
Dr Chivers	43
Rope	83
Another Turned Page	94
Stone Tapes	119
Best Served Cold	136
Mr Harland	145
Mole Vole and Duck	157
Homeward Bound	178
My Dearest Emillia	183
Something Overheard	199
Cloak	209

Fenja Hill

Ruth	67
The Water of Life	127
Breaking the Silence	150
What We Believe	172

Elizabeth Lawrence

The Sea Gives and the Sea Takes Away	17
Doctor	46
Doctor in the House	58
Rope	73
A Stitch in Time Saves Nine	96
Water My Blood	111

Macaque

Social Media	12
Poet's Retreat	25

_Honesty	37
Wrecking Ball	61
Down by the River	77
The Customer is always right	99
For the Record	107
In the Bag	138
Oxford, 1920	148
The Historians	160
K'Homun Umbrakai	169
Fields of Attraction	188
Day Tripper	197
In the Coppice Wood	205

Simon Phelps

When the Doctor Calls	52
Oliver Patterson's Adventurous Year	87

Brian Price

Dressing Up	24
A Peculiar Sighting	29
Time for the Doctor	49
An Unintended Consequence	71
Need to Know	101
A Slipped Disk	122
Payback	131
Customer Service	159
Train From Hell	176
Lamb for the Slaughter	185
Café au Hate	195
Lost Property	211

Acknowledgements

As a group we are grateful to Bari Sparshott for his wonderful bespoke sketches in each anthology, and to the various venues around Weston that have hosted our meetings, reserving tables for us, opening early to accommodate us, and even inspiring a monthly theme or two, including The Bay Café, Revo Kitchen and most recently Sanctuary games café. Finally, we are grateful to our readers for your support and encouragement.

Cant wait for the next anthology? Here is a taster...

A Safe Place

Macaque

Jordy

Rhope's eye, Rhope's eye, Rhope's eye, Rhope's eye.

Thorn

That's all Jordy been sayin' this last twoweek – "Rhope's eye, Rhope's eye," like a mantra or something. His own eyes be all glassy-lookin', too. I wish Ma was still with us. She'd get him right.

Leeza

They've taken Arthur up to the courthouse for firin' Pa's gun that night. This business got him all worked up, and he was feared for us lives. I guess we all was, really. We was all holed up in the house expectin' some wrongdoin' to come and befall us after dark.

Thorn

Art sat up every night with the gun loaded on his lap. He slept fitful in the day, and we all slept fitful at night. None of us could get our chores done or nothin'. And Jordy started talkin' about the eye bright as a blood moon. Sometimes I heard him talkin' to it. We was all just crazed up, you know. Then Art heard something out in the barn.

Leeza

I was awoke sudden in the night, there was a sound like someone smashin' up the barn. Then I heard the porch door open and Art call out, his voice was loud and strong but I could hear he was afeared. I heard him shout, then I heard the gun go off. Maybe I heard runnin' out behind the barn, but maybe alls I heard was Thorn on the staircase down to the kitchen.

Jordy

Rhope's eye, Rhope's eye, Rhope's eye, Rhope's eye.

Art

I hadn't seen John for a while. But he came to see me at the courthouse. He'd been busy, outa town, said he couldn't divulge any details, but just to trust him. Told me what I needed to say to the judge. That and nothing more. John said the judge might call Leeza and Thorn to hear their part of the story. He thought Jordy would be too young. Thing is, Jordy's been actin' so strange lately, he's like a shaman, and folks around here are real superstitious. Everybody's takin' an interest in Jordy, now.

Leeza

We got lanterns, me Art and Thorn, an' we went over to the barn real careful, like. In the shadows of the doorway there was this figure lyin' down. He w'nt movin' none.

Thorn

Arthur was turnin' around in circles, pointin' Pa's gun at the night. I held my lantern over the body, and there was blood all on his shirt front an' jacket. He was dead, alright, an' I said to Art, "Hell, you clean shot this feller," an he said "No I ain't. Alls I did was fire up into the sky to frightn'm off." So I waved my lantern back cross 'is face an' I said "Well, he's sure dead now. You think he fell outa the sky? Maybe he was up on the roof and you shot him off."

Leeza

None of us heard him come out the house behind us, but all a sudden Jordy says "he already dead when he got here. Just like the others. Rhope's eye sees all." Then he went back inside like there weren't no great spectacle to see out there, I mean like there weren't no dead man lyin just yards from our own porch. Man, he's really startin' to creep me out, that damn kid.

Arthur

The judge started by asking me about shooting the vagrant. Said he understood how we must've felt all alone out there with Ma and Pa gone, what with the recent accidents and all. I told him I didn't recall no accidents, just like John told me. John said to just say enough, let the judge unravel all the details slowly for himself and the court to hear. Judge said he could be lenient over the demise of a wanderin' theif, but he'd have to look for a better home environment for all us kids. Said we couldn't stay on the farm no more. I said I didn't kill no vagrant.

Thorn

When Jordy crept up on us in the dark and fair scared the you-know-what out of us, I took a closer look at the body. All the blood was near enough dried already, an though it had soaked through his clothes, there was none on the dirt around him. I put my hand to his face and he was dead cold already.

Leeza

Art said we should lock ourselves back inside till the mornin', then Thorn could go tell the sheriff, and he would find John. By the following afternoon, Art and Pa's gun were both locked up in town.

Art

I told the judge what an independent doctor had said about the body. Said I had his written testimony stored in a safe place. He asked about this doctor, and I said he was the same one who had written statements about Mr Rhope and Mr Cloke, and how their deaths were not the work of nature, nor had they been killed on our land. Then he wanted to know what that supposition had to do with me bein' held over on a charge of manslaughter, an' I said I thought it was obvious. It had to do with people wantin' our land. There was a murmur up in the gallery at that.

Thorn

When John came to see the body, he had some papers with him, and he wanted to take another look at the papers the men from town tried to get Arthur to sign on account of old Rhope dyin'. He told us that both Mr Rhope and Mr Cloke had taken out some sorta policy on their lands that neighbour ours, and now, since they've died, some big company owns the lot. 'Cept our bit in the middle. John reckoned that four more accidents happening to kids would look suspicious, so this company was now fixin' to scare us off our farm.

Art

I did what John said during the questioning. I made it clear that I had evidence put by in a place of safety, and it wasn't nowhere on the farm. I also pointed out that the fellers in the expensive suits up in the gallery were from the big city news firms, the nationals, and they were mighty interested in these events what's been happenin' on our land. John says it's hard to tell just who's involved, so we gotta play our hand careful and confident. Old judge did look kinda pale when I got talkin'. I just gotta trust John, I guess.

Jordy

Rhope's eye turnin' on its ugly thread. Light's gone out of it. Don't hear it talk no more. I think Old Rhope's work here's all done.